"The baby isn't yours," she said coldly

Alex was silent for a minute, his eyes searching her face, looking deeply into hers, their amber shaded by dark eyelashes. "Are you telling me the truth?" he grated.

"It's Casimir Rudenko's baby. That's why I left the ballet. I didn't want him to know."

Suddenly Alex raised both hands and tightened them into brutal fists as if he would hit her in his anger. Carrie cringed and backed away, frightened by the fury and loathing in his eyes. He saw the motion and gave a harsh laugh. "I don't hit women," he said through clenched teeth. "I've been brought up to be a damned gentleman."

"I'm sorry—" she began.

"The hell you are," he grated, his face bleaker than the gray sky above their heads. "The hell you are!"

Books by Claire Harrison

HARLEQUIN PRESENTS
671—PROPHECY OF DESIRE
705—DANCE WHILE YOU CAN

CLAIRE HARRISON

dance while you can

Harlequin Books

TORONTO • NEW YORK • LONDON
AMSTERDAM • PARIS • SYDNEY • HAMBURG
STOCKHOLM • ATHENS • TOKYO • MILAN

Harlequin Presents first edition July 1984
ISBN 0-373-10705-6

Original hardcover edition published in 1984
by Mills & Boon Limited

CHAPTER ONE

THE applause of two thousand five hundred people thundered over her as she bent in a deep curtsey, the sole figure on a wide stage, the white tulle of her tutu spread wide. She was Odette, the Swan Queen, in *Swan Lake*, and she knew that tonight had turned her into a star, but she trembled with fatigue and sweat was dripping down her cheeks. Her toes burnt in her shoes and her breath was ragged in her chest. Nearly twenty years of dancing made this triumph seem ephemeral, as if a dream had brushed her mind and she would wake up to find herself at the barre once more, every muscle strained beyond endurance.

Carrie stood hesitantly in the doorway of the hotel's dining room and lounge. It was an elaborate doorway made of heavy wrought iron grillework curved into an arch, and the room beyond it held the same feeling of quality and luxury. The floor was carpeted in deep blue; the glass chandeliers had been dimmed to a faint gold; and the candles set on each table cast flickering circles of light on to the white linen. During the day, the dining room had a utilitarian atmosphere, but at night when some of the tables had been moved to leave a space for dancing, and the sliding wall that divided the bar from the rest of the room was opened, the atmosphere became intimate, enticing, almost sensuous.

The lilting melody of a fifties foxtrot reached her ears, and she stepped forward to see the band. Three men, playing a piano, a saxophone and drums, stood under a spotlight in one corner. Before them couples swayed on the small dance floor while others watched from the tables, their faces white ovals in the semi-darkness. There was the occasional flare of a match or lighter which would illuminate a face, but then it would die away, leaving only the red-gold tip of a cigarette in the air.

The bar, Carrie noticed, had several men by it, and their quick glances in her direction made her nervous. She walked through the room, ignoring the looks that followed her slender figure in its flame-red dress, and passed through the French doors at the other end on to a wide patio. Beneath it lay the beach of Naples, lit only by the ivory disc of the Florida moon. The sand stretched in either direction like a pale carpet, and the water of the Mexican Gulf, a brilliant aquamarine by day, was as dark as the night, except for the silvered reflection of the moon's beams.

Carrie ran her fingers along the railing of the patio and threw her head back slightly, letting the breeze play with the tendrils of her hair, a fall of honey-brown waves that reached half-way down her back. Even at night the Florida air was balmy; she hadn't worn a sweater over her dress, leaving her shoulders bare except for the thin straps of the bodice. Behind her she could hear the strains of music, the hum of voices and of low laughter. She had a sudden wistful longing to be inside, to be one of the crowd, to be an ordinary person who worked a nine-to-five job and had a social life.

Carrie looked out towards the almost indistinct horizon and sighed. Her choice had been made years ago, and recent events had taken her far beyond even her wildest dreams. She could no more get off the merry-go-round than a painted horse on its pole. She owed bits of herself to everyone: the company, her partner Casimir Rudenko and the public. She wondered what her adoring fans would think if they knew just how restless and unhappy she was.

She was just about to turn and leave when a figure

detached itself from nearby a large standing fern. 'Don't leave,' a deep voice said. 'You're far too picturesque.'

'I . . . I hadn't realised I was being watched,' she said, taken aback. The stranger's tall figure in its dark suit had blended in so perfectly with the night that Carrie hadn't realised she shared the patio with anyone else.

He walked towards her, lithe and athletic, his hair gleaming sable in the illumination of a string of coloured lamps. As he approached his white shirt turned from blue to pink to a pale green under their lights, and the shadows on his face altered and changed, at first outlining a straight nose, then wide-set dark eyes under heavy brows and finally a well-moulded mouth set in a strong jaw.

His eyes were scanning her face, and Carrie had a momentary rush of fear. Although the coloured lights were designed for decorative purposes, they threw enough light for her features to be visible, and she had a distinctive oval face with slanted amber eyes set in dark lashes. It was a face that had adorned posters, newspaper articles and television frequently enough in the past few months to make her familiar to strangers. Carrie stiffened against the railing, waiting for the inevitable comment, but when she realised that he hadn't recognised her, she relaxed slightly, letting her breath out and releasing the tension in her legs and back.

'You're new?' the stranger asked, leaning on the railing next to her.

'A guest for a few days,' Carrie answered, her heart beginning to thump in an odd sort of rhythm. She wasn't tall, only five feet three, and the stranger loomed over her, his shoulders wide and formidable.

He turned from her to look towards the Gulf. 'Do you think,' he said in a musing voice, 'that there's something magical about moonlight, palm trees and a sea breeze, or is it a damned cliché?'

Carrie gave him a quick, curious look. Although she

wasn't accustomed to meeting strange men on dark tropical nights, the scenario itself suggested an opening line far different from what had been spoken.

'It's a cliché,' she said.

He gave her a sideways glance. 'You're not a romantic?' he asked.

Carrie was beginning to enjoy this conversation. Fame, she had learned the hard way, brought both rewards and penalties. Dance companies wanted her for guest appearances; the most exciting roles in ballet were hers for the asking; there was even talk of a movie. But the other side of the coin was less rosy. Her privacy was precious but difficult to maintain, and she could only relinquish her guard among friends. She relished the freedom of saying what she wished to a stranger who had no idea of her identity.

'On the contrary,' she said with a smile, 'I'm an incredible romantic. I'm capable of swooning over a dozen red roses, and a kiss on the hand can make my pulse rate go off the charts!'

'It sounds alarming,' he said drily. 'Do you often require medical aid?'

Carrie shook her head. 'I carry smelling salts—standard equipment for a fainting heroine.'

His smile revealed strong white teeth and an indentation in one cheek. 'And when you're not swooning or shocking the medical establishment, what do you do?'

Carrie hesitated for a brief second. 'I work in advertising.'

'New York?'

She nodded. 'And you?'

'An energy consultant; I work for oil companies.'

'You must travel a lot,' she hazarded, guessing that he held some sort of senior position. He looked to be about thirty-five.

'I've been in Africa for the past year—Ethiopia.'

Carrie suddenly realised why he had not recognised

her; he had been away in a country where the Western press had a minimal impact. She gave an unconscious sigh of satisfaction. She had spent most of her vacation in a state of self-imposed solitary confinement. She had been so tired of being sought after, bothered by strangers who wanted her autograph, her time, her smile, and her glamour to rub off on them. Her yearning for anonymity, among other things, had led her to seek a vacation away from Manhattan and the company.

'My name,' the stranger was saying, 'is Alex Taylor.'

'I'm . . . Bonnie Hughes,' Carrie lied, giving a silent blessing to her room-mate who had made the reservation under her maiden name, thereby bestowing upon Carrie an innocuous identity that she fortified by wearing large sunglasses during the day and wearing her thick swathe of hair down instead of in its customary dancer's chignon.

'Do you dance, Bonnie Hughes?'

For a second she was on edge again, but then she realised that music from the band could be heard through the French doors and the stranger was only referring to ballroom dancing.

She tilted her head and smiled. 'When I'm in the mood,' she replied.

'And what kind of mood must that be?'

'The moon has to be at its zenith, the breeze has to carry the scent of the ocean and the lights have to be low.'

Alex Taylor was amused. 'Will any partner do, or do you have special requirements?'

Carrie had never realised how much she enjoyed a light flirtation. 'He has to be,' she mused, 'tall, not unattractive, and someone who won't step on my toes.'

Alex Taylor made a deep bow. 'At your service. I'm tall, have been told by several ladies that I am far from unattractive, and the last time I stepped on a girl's toes was in Mrs Jenkins' fifth grade dancing class.'

Carrie put on a severely judgmental expression. 'You do have the qualifications,' she agreed.

His voice was low. 'Will I pass?'

She stepped away from the railing and stood before him, looking up into his dark face. An odd shiver ran down her spine at the gleam in his eye, then she shrugged it off as the touch of a breeze on her bared back. 'You pass, Alex Taylor.'

The strains of music changed from a Latin beat to something slower and more languorous, and Carrie let herself be pulled into the stranger's arms. Despite his height and breadth they fitted together almost perfectly. Her head nestled under his chin; her cheek lay against the crisp white front of his shirt, the rhythm of the music augmented by the steady drumming of his heart. He had placed his hands on her waist and she rested hers delicately on his shoulders. As they circled, she could feel strong muscles move beneath the fabric of his suit, and their slight tensing sent a frisson through her.

'You're very light on your feet, Miss Hughes,' Alex Taylor murmured. 'I doubt if I could move fast enough to step on them.'

Carrie felt a bubble of laughter rising in her throat. 'Is that a compliment, Mr Taylor?'

He leaned back to look down at her, his dark eyes enigmatic between their lashes. 'When I compliment you, Miss Hughes, you won't need to ask.'

He pulled her closer, her slim form against his, and Carrie let herself be drawn into the magic of dancing with a handsome stranger on a moonlit night by the ocean. The patio could have been the stage for a romantic movie. The coloured lights softened the harsh edges of reality until nothing existed but the moment, the stranger's arms, and her own heady sense of freedom. She had been in the arms of so many men, dancers who had lifted her and handled her body, that she had become indifferent to anything but professional expertise. Now, she discovered that she could be highly sensitive to a masculine touch. She felt a sensual delight in the warmth of Alex Taylor's palm on her lower back and the way his hard, lean length pressed against her.

One dance merged with another. They talked occasionally, laughed a bit and Carrie felt as if she had drunk several glasses of champagne, not understanding that the high she was on from mutual attraction and moonlight could even be more dangerous than alcohol. When the band took a break, they moved into the lounge where they sat opposite one another in a tiny booth. Alex took her hands in his, and she could feel the strength of his fingers and their warmth as he caressed the sensitive skin of her wrist.

'What do you do in advertising, Miss Hughes?'

'Bonnie,' Carrie insisted with bubbly laughter.

'Bonnie,' he agreed, repeating the question. 'What do you do in advertising?'

By this time she had her story ready. 'I write copy,' she said airily. 'You know, using sex to sell soap and deodorants.'

'Are you good at it?'

'The sex or the soap and deodorants?' Carrie felt an inner glow of satisfaction at that remark. It was the sort of thing Bonnie would say, and Carrie had often watched, with a tinge of jealousy, the way her room-mate could twirl men around her little finger, each and every one succumbing to her laughing glance and quick wit. Even though she was only recently divorced, Bonnie already had half a dozen boy-friends.

'The sex.' The look Alex Taylor gave her was shrewd and appraising, but Carrie was so intoxicated by her ability to imitate Bonnie that the anser came easily to her.

'Oh, I'm terrific,' she said lightly.

His dark eyes glinted at her. 'Lots of practice?'

She tossed her head, giving him a meaningful look. 'As much as the next girl.'

The waiter arrived with two Piña Coladas. 'Mmmm,' said Carrie, sipping at the creamy coconut drink that was spiced with rum. 'It's good!'

Alex talked about his work in Ethiopia, making her laugh over his stories, and they exchanged the kind of information common to new acquaintances. Without quite noticing how it had happened, Carrie went through four Piña Coladas. Her amber eyes began to sparkle, and she felt vibrant and alive under Alex's obvious approval. The world took on a golden glow that seemed to settle around his head, and his handsome features drew her eyes constantly. She had the urge to run her hand along his lean cheek and stroke his hair which gleamed blue-black in the dim lights of the bar.

They danced again and again, this time mixing with other couples. Alex occasionally paused to look down into her radiant face, and once he kissed her gently on the lips, a soft brushing that made her quiver in response. He held her closer to him, and Carrie wrapped her arms around his neck, letting her body arch upwards to meet his in an unconscious invitation. She didn't notice the glint of desire in his eye; she only felt the appreciative tightening of his arms around her and smiled dreamily, her eyes closing, the dark lashes sweeping the flushed skin of her cheeks.

So lost was she to reality that she never questioned his right to lead her out of the lounge and into the elevator, and not even the realisation that they were on a different floor from her own room brought her to her senses. Instead, she tripped slightly as they left the elevator, giggling as he grabbed her arm.

'You're drunk,' he said.

She was; she could feel it in the humming of her ears and the way the walls of the corridor seemed to dip and sway before her. She was drunk on Piña Coladas, on not

being Carrie Moore for the night, and on romance. She
knew where the evening was headed and she welcomed
it with a giddy joy. Other women had seized the right to
pleasure, and for once in her life, Carrie was going to do
the same. Later, she would return to her real life, to the
constant classes and rehearsals, the press conferences
and interviews, and the ever-present apprehensions that
had haunted her since the star of her success had taken
its meteoric rise to the stratosphere. But for tonight, she
was free and ready for a moment created by music,
moonlight and the curve of a stranger's arms.

Alex opened the door to his hotel room, and Carrie
got a glimpse of a plush suite decorated in blues and reds
as he led her through the living room into the bedroom,
where a lamp gleamed in one corner, turning the satin
spread on the king-size bed into a shimmering sea of
gold. He let go of her, took a step towards the lamp and
switched it off, plunging the room into darkness. The
next thing Carrie knew, she was being lifted into his arms
and carried over to the bed where he placed her with a
surprising gentleness. The change from being vertical to
horizontal made her head spin, and for a second she was
too disorientated to realise that he was pulling his
clothes off and then sinking down beside her.

'You smell delicious,' he murmured, pulling her towards him.

For a second, the old Caroline Moore came back in
full force. Her hand touched the bare skin of his chest
with its covering of hair and pulled back as if burnt.
What was she doing, lying next to this naked stranger
whose mouth was parting her lips, seeking out its secret
warmth? For a moment, her body stiffened, and then
she forced herself to relax. She knew what she was
doing. She was being Bonnie Hughes, who would never
resist the advances of an attractive man whose sexual
appeal made her senses tingle in anticipation. Instead,
she would encourage them, allow the straps of her gown

to be pulled away from her shoulders and permit a dark head to descend to the swelling curves of her bared breasts, her breath gasping at the sudden pleasure of a man's gentle bite.

She buried herself in sensation, every nerve alive to the movement of Alex's skilled hands. Her dress was discarded over the side of the bed, the wispy lace of her underclothes disappearing as if all her life she had been meant to be naked on this bed, her legs entwined with his, her hands instinctively caressing his hard muscles. Alex groaned slightly and ran his fingers through the long swathe of her hair, wrapping it around his hand as if it were a rope. 'You could be a slave woman,' he said huskily, pulling her head back slightly so that the hollow of her throat was exposed to his mouth.

'Could I?' she whispered, staring up at the white oval of his face.

'Mmm,' he murmured against her skin, 'I'll make you beg!'

Carrie, intoxicated by the feel of his lips on the pulse in her throat, gave a low laugh. 'For what?' she teased.

'Witch!' he responded. 'You'll find out.'

Time shifted, altered and pulsated as his hands and mouth stroked the slim circle of her waist, her hips, and the soft curve of her thighs. Carrie learned that her body possessed an unsuspected degree of passion, an aching desire for fulfilment that made her moan and writhe in wanting until she did finally beg for release. And Alex at once complied, his own rough breathing mingling with hers, his possession total and utterly complete.

Sunlight played off the ceiling, the walls and the twisted sheets, illuminating Carrie's face and the tangles of her hair, bringing out glints of gold in its rich brown depths. She slept on her side, one hand under her cheek, a slim brown shoulder bare above the edge of the blanket. The man beside her was propped up on his elbow, his dark eyes watching her, his gaze thoughtful, puzzled and disturbed. He frowned, the dark brows pulling in a straight line across his broad forehead, and his mouth tightened. Then as if coming to a sudden decision, he flung the sheets away and got out of bed, the tanned, muscular length of his body throwing a shadow across Carrie's face.

She blinked twice, closed her eyes again and then turned over on her other side, groaning slightly. Her eyes seemed to be glued together, her head was pounding unmercifully and her tongue felt swollen in her mouth. She had never felt quite so wretched, and she blinked again, forcing her eyes to remain open despite the painful searing of sunlight on their sensitive surface.

'Here, try this.'

A dark, lean hand appeared in her range of vision, proffering a glass of ice water and an aspirin, and she sat up, holding the sheet across her bare breasts, and accepted them with murmured thanks. The cold water was like a balm, and when she finished drinking, she held the glass up to her forehead, letting its frosty surface soothe the pain in her head, her eyes closing so she could concentrate on its healing qualities.

'Where am I?' she asked.

'In my room.'

Carrie's eyes snapped open and focused on the man lounging on the chair beside the bed. He wore a pair of jeans and nothing more. The sunlight brought out the mahogany sheen of his chest and its triangle of dark hair angling to his waistband. The planes of his face were strong and his features well formed, his black hair tousled as if someone had run their fingers through its thick strands.

'I . . . slept here,' she said. 'Didn't I?'

He nodded in affirmation. 'Snored, even.'

'I don't snore!'

He grinned. 'Sorry, I must have been dreaming.'

Carrie put the glass down and clasped it with both hands, her knuckles whitening. 'We made love,' she said flatly. It was all coming back to her, in every excruciating detail.

His mouth twisted in amusement. 'I'd be insulted if you didn't remember!'

She stared at his handsome face and bit her lip, a hollow, awful feeling in the pit of her stomach. The romance of the evening before had all but evaporated in the light of morning, as she realised what she had lost and at what cost. Everything that she held dear; her past, her beliefs and her discipline, had just been carelessly tossed away in a stranger's arms. A stranger! A man she didn't know about whose dark eyes now watched in an almost clinical fashion as if he were undressing her still or, even worse, remembering what had happened the night before.

Carrie stared again at the glass in her hands, suppressed the cry that wanted to tear out of her and felt her throat swell in despair. She had no heart for this charade, for the morning-after reality that being Bonnie imposed on her. She didn't want to act flirtatious or carefree. She felt sick and empty and wanted to sink into a dark oblivion where no one could find her and know her shame. If only . . . if only . . . she felt tears pricking behind her eyelids . . . if only she hadn't lied so recklessly! If only she'd been honest with herself and Alex, then none of this would have happened.

She glanced at him through her lashes, then blushed at her own rush of memory as her eyes fell to the lean hands which rested on his jean-clad legs. As a lover Alex had been gentle and thoughtful, passionate and fervent. His fingers had been skilful and knowing, he had roused her to heights of sensuality that she hadn't known she possessed. It could have been different; he could have been violent or abusive or demanding. Instead, he had pleased her, and she had no right to condemn him for

taking advantage of her own willingness. Carrie suddenly felt a pang of guilt. She had led him on and used him
sexually to experiment, to break out of the mould that
was strangling her. The least she could do was apologise
and confess. Once she did, she knew he would understand and they could part in a cordial fashion. She could
go on with her life and he could go on with his.

It seemed such a reasonable course of action that
Carrie felt a great wash of relief and she gave Alex a
smile that was unconsciously brilliant. 'Oh, I remember,' she said.

A strange expression of bitterness passed fleetingly
over his face, but he leaned forward and tweaked her on
the nose. 'Good,' he said lightly. 'I'm macho enough to
prefer that a woman doesn't forget me.'

Carrie cleared her throat. 'I think I'd better . . .' she
began, but he cut her off.

'We have a game of tennis, lunch and then an afternoon's sailing.'

Her amber eyes widened. 'We do?'

Alex gave her an amused glance. 'Did you think that
we'd shake hands and call it a night?' he asked.

'I thought . . .' her voice faltered. That was exactly
what she had envisioned; a calm parting of the ways as if
they had never met or known one another intimately,
but now she saw that Alex had something far different in
mind. Whether she liked it or not, she had made love,
participated in it, enjoyed it, and knew that the man
sitting so nonchalantly beside her would expect her to do
it again. Unhappily, she recognised that the act of love
had given him a sense of possession. She was his for the
duration of his stay, and she suddenly realised what the
truth of her identity would give him; the right to pursue
her if he wished, the belief that he could possess her
again. With a sinking heart, Carrie understood what she
must do: the charade she had begun so brazenly the
night before would have to be played out in full.

'Thought what?' he asked.

She swallowed with difficulty. 'That we'd have breakfast first.'

'I see.' One eyebrow arched mockingly. 'You're hungry after last night?'

The sexual innuendo was obvious, but Carrie recklessly ignored the clamour of her conscience and the stinging of her unshed tears and forced her mouth into an arch smile. 'Very,' she said, her tone as light and as flirtatious as she could make it. 'I'm absolutely starving!'

Throughout the rest of the day, Carrie wavered between leaving Naples that night or staying the full term of her vacation, which meant one more day and night. Alex didn't make the decision easy. He was charming and the perfect companion. His tennis was far better than hers, but he was gallant enough to concede an occasional defeat. They lunched at a tiny bistro in the small town of Naples and their conversation was lighthearted and inconsequential. Sailing was a new sport to Carrie, and once they were out far enough in the small rented catamaran, Alex taught her how to take the tiller, laughing when she led them into the wind and the sails fluttered and then collapsed.

Alex had, Carrie noticed, an ability to enjoy himself without restraint that she envied. From the hints that he let drop, she suspected that the year in Ethiopia had been mostly hard labour and little pleasure. His work seemed to be like that; he freelanced for oil and gas companies, trouble-shooting wherever he was sent. Between jobs, he believed in playing as hard as he had toiled, and she wished she could emulate his carefree attitude. Nothing could stop her from feeling like a lazy truant when she missed the daily company class. All those years of constant practice at the barre had instilled a work ethic in her that never knew when to quit.

Still, the pleasure Alex took from the small details of

his day made her have a new perspective on her vacation. As they sat on the beach, sunning beside the
glittering blue Gulf, he pointed out the pelicans that
were flying by, their bills full of fish. He was an avid
collector of shells, and Carrie learned about the conches
that could be found only in the early hours of the
morning crawling at the shoreline, their shells golden-
brown on the outside, salmon-pink to purple inside.

He made her smile; he made her laugh, and Carrie
allowed herself to be lulled and enchanted until it was
too late to get on the flight back to New York. They had
dinner in the hotel's elegant dining room, and she didn't
need to be told that Alex approved of her black sheath
with its deep V-neckline or the slit up the side of the skirt
that showed the long length of her tanned leg. His dark
eyes said it all in one appreciative glance as he took her
arm. And she had to admit that he was pretty dazzling
himself. The dark tuxedo didn't hide the breadth of his
shoulders or the narrowness of his hips, and his tall
figure drew the gaze of other women.

The pattern of the evening was the same as the night
before except that, this time, they danced even closer,
his lips placing soft kisses at the sensitive chord by her
ear, and he murmured sweet nothings that made a flush
come over Carrie's cheeks. The awareness of what was
to come heightened every moment and every sensation.
She could feel the strong muscles of his chest through the
starched ruffles of his shirt and his fingers on her bare
spine made her quiver in anticipation. Sexual attraction,
she discovered, was a drug with its own potent form of
addiction. She didn't need to imagine that she was
Bonnie for this night. It was enough to be Caroline
Moore in the arms of a man who could arouse her by the
slanting glance of his dark eyes.

Their lovemaking that night was long, tender and
passionate. Carrie had avoided alcohol, only sipping at
her glass of champagne, and she came to him without

any senses altered or dulled. One night's experience had already taught her how to please him, and imagination did the rest. This time, she touched him until he moaned, his pitch of intensity equalled by hers.

The next day they sunned on the beach before she had to pack and leave for the airport. Carrie was on her stomach, letting the rays of the sun warm her back. She was in a narrow sea-green bikini, and she had braided her hair into a long plait that lay on one shoulder. Alex was applying suntan lotion to her legs and the circling motion of his hands had her dreamily content, almost mindless, as if nothing mattered beyond the strength of his fingers on the long line of her calves. When his voice came, she was so far away that she barely caught the implication of his words.

'Your fragility is deceiving.'

She opened her eyes and caught him staring at her legs, his hand resting on the muscle at the back of her knee.

'Your skin is soft,' he continued musingly, 'but underneath the muscles are . . .' He broke off. 'I would swear that you have the legs of a dancer.'

Carrie's mouth went dry. So far she had had no trouble maintaining her charade as Bonnie Hughes. In fact, she could have sworn that Alex was just as eager to keep their relationship at a level too superficial for deep digging into one another's lives. It was as if they had made a pact for these two days, an agreement that their affair was a fling, a shipboard romance on solid ground that wouldn't weather an everyday existence. She had been able to keep her lies to a minimum, talking about her job without identifying the company she worked for and where she lived without mentioning the street. The game had gone too far for her to give up now.

'I jog,' she said lightly.

'You like to exercise?'

It was easy to say the words, to give them a sexual

innuendo that would put off his questioning. 'All kinds,' she said with a smile.

He grinned and rolled over on to his back, his body taut and lean in black briefs. 'Frequently?' he asked.

'No comment,' she said. 'I plead the Fifth.'

'Coward,' he accused her lazily, and closed his eyes against the sun.

Carrie gave an inward sigh of relief and prayed that the afternoon would pass quickly. She glanced at his profile, appreciating the strong line of his jaw and the way his dark lashes lay against his bronzed skin. Most of the women she knew would consider her a mad fool. Alex was handsome, charming and a wonderful lover, not a man to be forgotten. But that was exactly what Carrie intended to do. A long-term love affair had no place in her life, and besides, when she dwelt on what had happened between them, she was filled with guilt and shame. She had lied through her teeth and slept with a stranger. Every scruple and moral principle that guided her life had succumbed to an overdose of sea, sand and moonlight.

Carrie resisted an urge to run her fingers through the dark hairs on Alex's bare chest. It was as if, she thought ruefully, she had been bewitched, put under a spell, altered from the person she was into someone she had never known. For hours at a time, Alex had made her forget that she was a dancer, that she faced a summer with the awesome task of learning three new ballets choreographed specifically for her, and that her life was driven by other people's demands and schedules to the point that she no longer knew what she herself wanted.

Unconsciously, she heaved a sigh and sat up, shading her eyes to watch some children who were playing at the edge of the water. There was a chubby little girl dressed in a blue playsuit and frilly white hat wielding a shovel with abandon, sending damp sand in every direction. Carrie smiled wistfully, wondering if she would ever

marry and have children. Other dancers had, but sometimes at the sacrifice of their career. Gregory Dunne, the
ballet-master, told all his dancers that 'husbands ruined
concentration and babies ruined bodies.' Carrie looked
down at her own slender waist and judged that five days
of eating and drinking had taken its toll. She would have
to go back on a diet tomorrow. Like every dancer she
was plagued by the need to remain as thin as possible.
Casimir would know if she had gained a pound; he was
the one who had to catch and lift her. He knew her body
almost as intimately as Alex did.

That thought made her grimace and she began to pack
up her beach bag.

'Tired of the sun?' Alex asked, leaning on her elbow.

'My plane leaves in two hours,' she said.

'You don't have to rush. I'll drive you to the airport.'

Carrie looked at him in surprise. 'You don't have to.'

'Maybe I want to,' he said wryly.

'Oh.'

'"Oh,"' he mimicked. 'Something tells me, Bonnie
Hughes, that you're good at starting affairs, but not
good at ending them.'

Carrie was glad that the sun had given a bloom to her
cheeks that hid their blush. She would have liked to
confess that she had little experience in either direction,
but instead she said blithely, 'I hate agonised partings.'

'Love 'em and leave 'em?' Alex suggested.

Carrie shrugged. 'Something like that.'

'You're a very tough lady,' he said sarcastically.

'Do you think it's only the male prerogative?' She
turned away and put on her sunglasses.

Alex ran a finger down her spine and hooked it around
the fastening of her bikini top. 'I think it's ugly in either
sex,' he said quietly.

Carrie stiffened at both his touch and his words. She
didn't like to sound jaded and sophisticated to the point
of being brittle, but she couldn't see any way of ending

this without being either nonchalant or brutal, and Alex was quickly pushing her in the latter direction. 'Sorry,' she said.

Suddenly he pushed her back down on to the blanket and pulled off her glasses, staring into her frightened amber eyes. 'I would have sworn,' he grated through clenched teeth, 'that you were different.'

Carrie swallowed. His broad shoulders blocked the sun and his mouth was set in a hard line. 'You learn something new every day,' she said flippantly, hoping that the tremor in her voice wasn't obvious.

The dark eyes ran over her face and then down to the top of her bikini, which barely held in the curves of her small, high breasts. 'Yes,' Alex said bitterly. 'I've learned that a woman can sleep with a man for the first time and act as if it were nothing.'

So he had known! Carrie cringed inwardly when she realised how she must appear to him; as a liar, a hypocrite and worse. There were names, all of them uncomplimentary, for a woman who tumbled into bed with the most available man like an animal in heat. Still, she saw no point in confessing now. She was going back to New York; Alex was flying out the next day for Los Angeles. They were ships that had passed in the night, nothing more and nothing less. She gritted her teeth and tried to erase all expression from her face. 'It had to happen some time,' she said airily.

Anger twisted Alex's mouth and caused his eyes to narrow. Muscles bunched powerfully in his upper arms and, for a second, Carrie had the horrible feeling that he might hit her. Then he pushed himself away and stood up, his body tall and dark, its lean lines outlined by the sun. He gazed down at her for a long moment in a mocking, derisive glance that made Carrie want to cover herself as if her body was dirty and shameful. She had an almost overwhelming urge to tell him the truth, to let him know that for her the past few days had been momentous, and that her initiation into the mysteries of sex had been as traumatic as it had been wonderful, but she said nothing, merely lifting her chin and staring back at him, forcing her eyes to be blank and emotionless like stones of amber.

'Have a good trip, Miss Hughes,' he said at last, in a tone that made her blood run cold. 'It was . . .' the pause was intentional, 'nice knowing you.'

He turned on his heel and walked away, never once looking back. Carrie sat up and watched him go, trying desperately to consider their parting as satisfactory. As far as she could see, the affair had to end, and it made no real difference whether it ended on a pleasant note or not. She was never going to see Alex Taylor again. What did she care if he despised her? She began to gather up her belongings and tried to think ahead. She had rehearsal tomorrow for a new ballet; she should go shopping for some summer clothes; she owed a letter to her parents. There were, she decided, enough things coming up to keep her very busy. Her life was full and she had lots of friends. She liked the way she lived and wouldn't change it for the world. How many other ballerinas were stars at twenty-two? How many women could claim that they had achieved the apex of success? It was all so wonderful that Carrie wondered why she wasn't ecstatic with happiness. She wondered why she was still sitting on the beach towel, her slender shoulders hunched over, tears dripping into her hands like falling rain.

CHAPTER TWO

'So? Who is he?'

'Who?'

Bonnie gave Carrie a look that was both concerned and shrewd and sipped at her coffee. 'The man, baby, the man!'

They were sitting, both in their bathrobes, in the breakfast nook of the kitchen, a bright room where the sun slanted through blue and white gingham curtains on to the butcher block table and a shelf of jams and jellies. Carrie reached for the butter dish and then put it down again. No more butter, ice cream or desserts. She had returned from Florida two days ago, but she still hadn't got over the luxurious habit she had developed on her vacation of eating whatever she wanted. It was funny, she thought to herself, how easy it was to become accustomed to excess and how difficult to adjust to starvation. 'What man?' she asked, taking a bit of unbuttered toast and grimacing at its flat flavour.

'The man you met in Florida.'

Carrie deliberately kept her eyes on the morning newspaper and avoided looking at Bonnie. Her roommate, she knew, had a nose for unearthing the most deeply buried secrets. 'I didn't meet anyone in particular,' she said casually.

'Hmm,' Bonnie tilted her head for side to side, her blonde cap of hair shining under the kitchen lights, and appraised Carrie as if she were a piece of merchandise. 'That's funny.'

Carrie finally looked up. 'What's funny?'

'I could have sworn . . .'

'Sworn what?'

'That all those heartfelt sighs, sudden blushes and shadows under the eyes all added up to the aftermath of a little vacation fling.'

Carrie looked away from Bonnie's inquisitive stare. She hadn't realised that she'd been so obvious. Why, she wondered desperately, couldn't she be like other women? Like Bonnie, who could throw off a boy-friend without a qualm and chalk up an affair to experience? From the moment that she had returned, Carrie had tried to take a blasé and nonchalant stance about what she had done in Florida, but she had found it wasn't that easy. Alex Taylor was never far from her mind. His face loomed up at her at the most inappropriate moments, and at night her body was haunted by the memory of his hands. 'You're imagining things,' she said, but the lack of conviction in her voice made Bonnie lean forward.

'A hot, torrid affair,' she said with a smile. 'That's what I'm imagining.'

Carrie sighed in resignation; she knew from past experience that there was no stopping Bonnie when she had a goal in sight. The other girl had a streak of persistence that verged on fanatical. What Bonnie wanted, Bonnie got, and nothing Carrie could say or do would alter that. 'There was someone,' she admitted at last.

'Aha,' said Bonnie, her blue eyes gleaming with satisfaction. 'I knew it!'

Carrie poured herself a cup of black coffee and took a sip.

'Well?'

'Well what?'

'Carrie, I could wring your neck! Come on, spill the beans. What was he like? Tall, short, fat, skinny, gorgeous?'

Carrie took another bite of toast. 'Good-looking.'

Bonnie closed her eyes in exasperation. 'Fair, dark, a

redhead? For heaven's sake, didn't you at least get his vital statistics?'

Carrie choked a bit on her toast. She knew far more about Alex Taylor's vital statistics than she was willing to admit to anyone. 'It was just a . . . short-lived romance,' she said. 'Nothing that I plan to lose any sleep over.'

Bonnie looked at her in disbelief. 'Are you going to see him again?'

Carrie shook her head.

'Why not?'

'I'm too busy. I can't afford any emotional entanglements.'

'That career of yours is interfering with your life,' Bonnie scolded.

'Dancing is my life,' Carrie countered indignantly.

Bonnie shook her head in disgust. 'You're far too solitary, Carrie. It isn't healthy.'

'Since when were you an advocate for long-term boy-friends?' Carrie asked in astonishment.

Bonnie threw her hands up in the air. 'Okay,' she said, 'I deserve that, but you're at the other extreme. You don't go out at all. It's a lopsided sort of life.'

Carrie set her mouth in a stubborn line. 'I don't want to do anything but dance,' she insisted.

Bonnie sighed in resignation. 'You dancers are all a little crazy, did you know that?'

Later, as she dressed to go to the ballet studio, Carrie reflected on Bonnie's last words. Dancers had to be slightly insane, she supposed. The work was excruciatingly hard, the pay was mediocre and the only real rewards were in the dancing itself. Even Bonnie, who worked for the ballet company and knew far more about dancers than most people, could not really understood the drive and determination that had kept Carrie going since she had been three years old.

Carrie had been barely walking and out of diapers when her parents had first noticed her desire to dance whenever there was music on the stereo or radio. They had taken moving pictures of her waltzing around the living room, her tiny chubby face wearing a far away expression, her little body already moving in a complicated rhythm. When she was six, her mother had finally yielded to Carrie's pleas for lessons and she was enrolled in a small school in their San Francisco suburb. By ten, Carrie was starring in recitals and by the time she was fifteen, it was obvious to everyone that her future was in ballet. A year later, she auditioned for the Manhattan Ballet Company and joined as a student.

Living in New York had, at first, been a frightening experience for Carrie, who was accustomed to a quiet neighbourhood with her family around her. She had moved into the dormitory of the ballet school, at first sharing the room with another aspiring dancer and then being left on her own when the other girl dropped out. The hustle and bustle of the city, the fierce ambitions of her fellow dancers and her own shyness combined to create a solitary existence. The only time she was truly happy was when she was dancing. Then she could bury her fears and loneliness in the music and the fluid movements of her body.

She graduated from the ballet school and joined the corps de ballet, coming under the guidance of Gregory Dunne, the choreographer and ballet-master. He was the one who had noticed the small girl in the ranks with the large amber eyes whose line was extraordinarily pure and whose dancing had an unusual depth of passion. He moved her, at first, into small roles, letting her gain experience, and chose her as an understudy for Veronica Timberlane, the company's senior ballerina. Her break came when Veronica was laid up by a severe 'flu and Carrie had taken her place as the Swan Queen in *Swan Lake*. It had been almost incomprehensible to her that she—Caroline Moore—standing alone on stage, her arms filled with flowers, could cause that excitement, that roar in the audience and wildly enthusiastic clapping. All she had done, she had thought, trembling from exhaustion and nerves, was dance.

'I'm leaving,' Bonnie called through her bedroom door. 'Do you want to share a taxi with me or be a sardine in the subway?'

'I'm coming!' Carrie hurried out of her room, dressed in her usual jeans and T-shirt, a bag of practice clothes slung over one shoulder, and met Bonnie at the door of the apartment. Her room-mate as usual looked as if she had stepped out of a bandbox. 'New suit?' she asked, admiring the dark blue ultra-suede outfit that Bonnie was wearing with a white silk blouse and mauve chiffon scarf.

'I picked it up while you were in Florida.'

'It's gorgeous,' Carrie said with sincerity. In addition, to having a lovely classical line, the suit's rich blue colour emphasised Bonnie's blonde looks.

'Thanks.' Bonnie threw the bolt on the apartment door. 'I had a few extra dollars burning a hole in my pocket.'

Carrie gave her room-mate an indulgent smile. A few extra dollars to Bonnie was a fortune to others. In the Hughes family, money was like water that flowed in a steady stream from a fountain of inherited wealth. Carrie had never quite plumbed the depths of Bonnie's finances, but she knew from an occasional glance at the mail that the other girl could have lived quite well on her investments. But Bonnie wasn't the kind of person who liked to be idle. She had energy, spirit and enthusiasm to burn. She didn't, she had once told Carrie, have the right personality to be a jet-setter. 'Hours of nothing to do except visit the couturiers and hairdressers and gossip,' she had said with a shudder. 'It just isn't my style.'

Bonnie had been hired as an assistant publicity director to the Manhattan Ballet Company four years before when it was seeking to change its image from purely classical to innovative and expand its repertoire. She had been chosen, not because she had any experience in public relations, in fact she hadn't, but because she came from a high stratum of New York society that gave her impeccable and prestigious connections to help the company get private funding. In addition to being born with a golden spoon in her mouth, Bonnie Hughes Devitt at eighteen had married the heir to the international firm of Devitt Chemicals.

'Mark and I were like two children playing house,' she had once confided to Carrie. 'Our parents threw us together, hormones did the rest, and suddenly I was married to a man I barely knew and frankly didn't like all that much. To be honest, we were both spoiled brats.'

Although Bonnie knew the reasons behind her hiring, she had been determined to make a success of her first job. One of her earliest projects had been developing Carrie as a public figure, and she had been instrumental in getting small articles about her in the press. Despite the four-year difference in their age and experience, Carrie and Bonnie had become friends. Carrie enjoyed Bonnie's sense of humour and down-to-earth pragmatism that could reduce even the most troublesome problem to a reasonable size. Since they were opposites, their attraction was mutual. When Bonnie's marriage, already rocky, finally fell apart, she asked Carrie to move in with her, saying that she hated being alone.

Living with Bonnie had taught Carrie a great deal beyond the claustrophobic world of the dancer. She learned about the elegance and sophistication that comes with having more than enough money to spend. Bonnie's apartment was indecently large for even a pair of room-mates. While most New Yorkers scrambled for apartments, barely affording rooms the size of closets, Bonnie lived in an elegant building on the upper West Side and had a four-bedroom flat with a den, music room and studio where she painted.

Bonnie taught her how to dress, wear her hair and use make-up. She knew every secret in the book and used them. Although she wasn't pretty by ordinary standards, her face was a bit too angular, her nose too long, Bonnie was able to create the image of a striking, flamboyant woman who had a flair for clothes and a sense of high style. Her fair hair was cut into a geometric cap and her blue eyes, her best feature, were always highlighted until they dominated her face. Men, Carrie had noticed, never seemed to realise that Bonnie wasn't the most beautiful woman in the room. They were drawn to her as if she were a glittering, iridescent gem.

'Have you started work on Gregory's new ballet?'

Carrie's thoughts were pulled back to the present as the taxi roared through the early morning traffic and pulled up before the ballet school. 'We started on Monday.'

'And the pas de deux with Casimir?'

'Today.'

Bonnie paid the cabby and said as they both got out, 'I might have the photographers come and take some pictures of you and Casimir rehearsing. It sounded good on paper.'

Carrie shifted her heavy bag on to her other shoulder as they walked through the front door. 'Casimir will love that,' she said dryly.

Bonnie gave her an amused look. 'Dear Casimir,' she said. 'What would we do without him?'

'Have some peace?' Carrie suggested.

Bonnie gave her a supportive pat on the shoulder as they parted. 'Peace isn't good for publicity.'

Bonnie knew her business, Carrie reflected later as she stood in the doorway of the studio and watched Casimir putting on his usual act. Several guests of Gregory's had come to watch the rehearsal, and Casimir, the first to arrive, was entertaining them with grand leaps and turns. The visitors were enthralled by this unexpected performance, gratification on their faces. Casimir, of course, looked as if he hadn't even noticed his audience, but Carrie knew better. His ego was the size of the national debt and craved attention of any kind. He was a scene-stealer and a show-off, and the only thing that saved him from ostracism by his fellow dancers was his marvellous Russian technique and exuberance. He was good; he knew it, they knew it and the ballet devotees knew it. From the moment he had defected to the United States, there had been a mutual love affair between Casimir and his public.

He was a big man with big appetites, a blond handsome giant with a wide Slavic face and blue eyes that expressed every emotion in outrageous exaggeration. He loved to dance and was enormously strong. Carrie had never had a partner who lifted her so easily, as if she were made of airy feathers instead of bone and sinew. He had a flamboyant, boyish charm that made women's hearts melt like wax in the sun. He had had affairs with almost the entire corps de ballet, going through girls like a fast racing car eating up miles. The extraordinary thing about his sexual escapades was that he rarely made an enemy. His past lovers still responded to his flirtations as if they hoped for a repeat performance, and the women yet to come seemed to line up for the honour.

So far as Carrie knew only two women in the ballet company had refused him. The first was Veronica, whom he had partnered during his first few years in the United States. They fought like cats and dogs over everything from a dance step to its interpretation, Veronica insisting that flashy technique had nothing to do with competence and Casimir calling her out-of-date and hidebound by tradition. The partnership had foundered more than once while Gregory desperately sought ways to soothe tempers and troubled waters. When Carrie had taken Veronica's place, she had also been paired with Casimir. Part of her success had been their 'rightness' as a couple.

Casimir had immediately assumed that they would become lovers, but Carrie had refused every pass he had thrown her way. He had acted like a stricken animal when she refused, trying to snow her under with his Russian impetuosity. He had sent her flowers, argued passionately and teased her unmercifully, even whispering seductive messages in her ear while they were dancing before an audience. Carrie would merely smile, pat his cheek and slip out of his embrace. She admired him and loved to dance with him, but he was far too much like an overgrown child for her to take him seriously. When he had realised that she couldn't be budged, Casimir had taken off again on his pursuit of the corps de ballet, but every once in a while he would take another flyer in her direction just to keep his hand in. To Carrie's annoyance, this morning was obviously going to be one of those times.

'Sweetheart!' Casimir came up and, wrapping his arms around her waist, lifted her in the air and swung her around three times, his muscles bulging under the stretchy material of his leotard. 'You had a good vacation?' He nuzzled her neck, murmuring endearments in Russian.

'Yes. Please put me down.'

He obediently returned her to the floor but kept his arms around her for the benefit of the visitors. 'So beautiful,' he whispered. 'Lovely brown skin and golden eyes. You are a sun nymph, *lapushka*.'

Carrie tried to push his arms away. 'There's no such thing.'

He ignored her efforts. 'No such thing as what?'

'As a sun nymph.'

'Ah,' he breathed, his blue eyes suddenly passionate, 'for you, I create one.'

'Casimir!' Carrie warned.

To her infinite relief, Gregory returned and clapped his hands, causing Casimir to let her go. Several other dancers who were part of the scene drifted into the studio and deposited their bags under the bench. The room began to take that look and feel of ballet that Carrie loved. She enjoyed rehearsals, when a new idea for a ballet was slowly developed and unfolded, the choreographer's vision adapting to the dancers' abilities, the unique talents of the dancers subtly altering the dance itself.

Gregory discussed the scene and explained the meaning of the pas de deux, his fat pudgy hands moving in graceful gestures in the air. He was a short, heavy man who was incredibly light on his feet, a former dancer in the eons ago when he had been thin and had a full head of hair. Now he was bald, fat and inclined to chew on a cigar as he worked.

'Do you understand that, Carrie? You are a young girl in love who doesn't understand what this emotion is all about. You are frightened, virginal, ready to flee when Casimir approaches. He is hard and tough, a fighter who is intent upon getting his way. The whole of the ballet has led up to this pas de deux, this conflict and your ultimate surrender. I want feeling here, lots of emotion.'

Carrie nodded as he went on to talk to the other dancers. She leaned forward and retied one of the ribbons on her pink pointe shoes, a slim figure in a black leotard and tights. A sense of excitement was in her. She had spent the previous two days working on other parts of the ballet, her first solo and an enchanting scene where she was surrounded by friends who were helping her dress for a date. It was a modern piece with age-old themes of love and betrayal. She could already feel herself in the part, being the girl. It didn't matter that the studio held the faint scent of sweat from many hours of rehearsals or that the other dancers were dressed in their usual assortment of odd-coloured leotards, tights and leg-warmers. She could envisage this scene: lit in soft white, herself in a pale flowing chiffon, Casimir in black.

The beat of the music drew her up, and she and Casimir began the steps that would bring them together. She acted shy, evasive and uncertain. Casimir stalked, strong and forceful; his part strenuous and difficult, involving many leaps and jumps. Another dancer, playing the role of a friend, egged him on, inciting him until the studio rang from the rapid tempo of Casimir's feet on the wooden floor.

Then they were dancing together. Carrie turned to run, her feet on delicate pointes, her body arched in fear, but it was too late. She was caught, lifted like an exultant trophy, and they . . .

'Now,' said Gregory, waving his cigar in the air, 'it is at this moment when the music changes, when this semi-rape becomes lovemaking, that you both must change, the characters softening. Carrie, first you must show us that the girl has been seduced, overwhelmed by the man's display of virility. He is strong, handsome and masterful. You must give in; let desire carry you away.'

It was far easier than she had expected: Alex Taylor had taught her well. She danced around Casimir, the movements of love coming naturally to her. *Bourrée, bourrée, pirouette, arabesque* . . . *Hold* for three and then *slide*, two, three; *turn*, two, three; let her hand fall on Casimir's shoulder, caress his cheek and then *turn*, two, three . . . Carrie danced on, artful, alluring, her body swaying seductively, her feet weaving a dance of desire.

The tape stopped and Carrie halted, blinking at the silence, breathing hard with her exertions, her face flushed, damp tendrils escaping from her chignon and sticking to her cheeks and temples. Everyone was staring at her; Casimir, Gregory, the other dancers, the visitors sitting forward on their chairs. Suddenly the studio was filled with the sound of spontaneous applause.

Carrie blushed and then, not knowing exactly how to act, made everyone a small, ironic bow. 'Please,' she said.

Gregory came over and put his arm around her slender shoulders. 'You were marvellous, darling. They just want to acknowledge it.'

Carrie gave an embarrassed shrug. 'I was just doing what you told me to.'

He kissed her cheek, his round face beaming. 'There is a world of difference between doing just what I say and dancing.' He gave her a little hug. 'Who knows? Maybe we'll create a little bit of history with this ballet.'

But it was Casimir who had the final word. He caught Carrie just as she was coming out from the studio, her bag over her shoulder. 'You're not the same,' he said angrily.

Carrie glanced at him uneasily. 'I haven't changed,' she said.

He took her elbow in his large hand and led her out of hearing range from the other dancers. 'There is a lover,' he growled in his Russian accent.

'Don't be ridiculous!'

His mouth pouted like that of a sulky child, and his blue eyes reproached her. 'For me you are a block of ice; for someone else you are boiling water.'

Carrie couldn't refrain from smiling at Casimir's less than complete command of the English language. It was one of his more endearing characteristics.

'You smile, *lubimaya*,' he said, frowning, 'but we dance together long enough for me to know.'

Carrie looked away. She knew what Casimir meant. Dancers could rarely really keep anything secret from their partners. She always knew when Casimir was angry or upset, or even pursuing another woman; she could sense it in the way he tensed his body or handled her.

They had spent hours together in positions just short of complete intimacy. Still, she didn't want him to know about Alex. If he thought that she was available for an affair, he would pressure her with even greater intensity. Casimir had told her more than once that partners should sleep together; it made their dancing that much better.

'I'd never take a lover,' she said lightly, trying to defuse his anger. 'I'm saving myself for you.'

As she had expected, Casimir was easily diverted. He couldn't resist any pandering to his ego and he thrived on flirtation. 'And when will that be, *milaya*?' he asked, smiling and leaning down over her, ready for a kiss.

She pushed him away and shook a warning finger in front of him. 'None of your business,' she said.

No more was said about Carrie's holiday for weeks. Bonnie took a flying vacation in August to Europe where her parents had a villa in the south of France. Casimir was too involved in rehearsals and a new flame, a little dancer who had recently graduated from the ballet school, to take an active interest in Carrie. The days passed with a regularity that was almost monotonous. Carrie was rehearsing not only the ballet with Casimir but also two short solo pieces that Gregory had choreographed especially for her. In addition to the rigours of learning two new parts, Veronica was teaching her some of the classical roles.

The older ballerina could be imperious, haughty and nasty, but Carrie had discovered that Veronica's first love was ballet and the company, and nothing stopped her from their promotion. She gave unstintingly of her time and her energy and was adamant that Carrie do the same.

'It is your responsibility,' she said one hot afternoon when Carrie stood drooping at the barre, 'to carry on the tradition.'

Carrie, visibly wilting, shook her head in fatigue. For some reason, she felt tired most of the time, barely reacting to the alarm in the morning and in bed and asleep before the sun went down at night.

Veronica stood up and came over to her. 'My time is almost over,' she said, putting her hand on Carrie's shoulder. 'You're next in line.'

Carrie stared into the older woman's lined face and dark eyes. Although her body was still trim and had youthful lines, her brown hair pulled back into its dancer's chignon was streaked with grey. Veronica was already over forty, reaching the age when most ballerinas gave up dancing. She had been a wonderful dancer in her time, electrifying two generations of ballet-lovers on both continents, but she was shrewd enough to realise that her body was no longer flexible enough for the demands of dancing and had announced her retirement that spring. Carrie, who had often seen her reduce other dancers to tears, was thankful that Veronica had always treated her well. If the older woman were jealous, it never showed. She had a strong, indomitable will and, recognising that Carrie was the next in succession, she was determined to make her a dancer worthy of the reputation of the company.

'I wonder if it's worth it,' Carrie murmured.

'Worth it?' Veronica's eyes flashed. 'Of course it's worth it. How can you even ask?'

Carrie stretched a bit, feeling a sharp pain in her toes and knowing she would find blisters tomorrow. 'I have no other life,' she said.

'If you're an artist,' Veronica said with emphasis, 'you can't have another life.'

Carrie sighed. 'Didn't you ever want a family, Veronica?'

Veronica's mouth twisted slightly. 'It wasn't to be.'

Carrie recalled early pictures of Veronica and her regal beauty. 'But surely,' she said with a frown, 'you must have been in love and wanted to have children.'

Veronica smiled gently. 'Take a lover, child. That's what I'd advise. It's far less complicated.'

It wasn't, Carrie thought later with a touch of irony, as if she really had any choice. Her life was so restricted that she rarely met men, and she knew from other dancers how difficult it was to have boy-friends outside of the dance world. They couldn't understand the tensions and demands of ballet or recognise that a dancer must often put the company first. Dancers tended to date one another, have affairs with one another, and if they married, it was to one another. All in all, she thought with a sigh, it was a very small, incestuous environment.

She had, of course, not heard from Alex. Not that she had expected that she would. Their parting had been very terminal, a cutting of the cord with a definite slash. Besides, he would have great difficulty tracking her down unless he happened to read about her in the papers, and he hadn't struck her as the kind of man who followed the ballet world. From the time of her return Carrie had worked hard at pushing the memories of her stay in Naples down and out of sight. She had always thought that love should come before a sexual relationship, that physical intimacy was meaningless without it. She was ashamed at having slept with a stranger at the drop of a hat and mortified by the charade she had played. She had used Alex and he had used her in a degrading exchange of desire. Never again, she vowed, would she allow such a thing to happen.

Still the memories kept returning like bad pennies, invading her dreams and making her shiver in the midst of the most innocuous activity. She could blame Alex Taylor for several burnt dinners and one rehearsal when her ability to concentrate was so undermined by images of his face that Gregory had suggested rather sarcastically that she go home and recover from whatever ailed her.

She had reluctantly returned to the apartment, lay down on the sofa and slept for four hours, only to discover upon waking that she still felt tired and drained.

Nausea hit in mid-August and Carrie, already dieting, lost even more weight. She had no interest in foods that usually made her mouth water and, at one party held by a dancer friend, she took one look at the Mexican tacos and ran to the bathroom, her hand over her mouth. Her cheekbones took on a new dimension and her air of fragility increased to the point that even Veronica took pity on her, suggesting that she relax a bit and take it easy.

But Carrie drove herself even harder, refusing to give in to what she saw as a case of nerves and depression. She couldn't let two nights in a stranger's arms ruin her career. The company was to go on tour in the beginning of September with the new ballet and she intended to go with them. Their first stop was to be in San Francisco, and she would be able to visit her parents and her sister, whose new baby she hadn't yet seen. With that goal in mind, she strove to perfect her part in Gregory's ballet, to give it that extra edge that would make the dance memorable.

Costume fittings were held in the last week of August, and Carrie descended to the depths of the building where Mrs Martinelli dominated over the sewing room. The scene was one of frenetic activity, with three seamstresses working on costumes and one ironing and pressing, the hot steam already adding to the tropical temperature. Carrie had always liked the costume room, where each outfit reminded her of a certain ballet or part. There was the gold and white brocaded tutu of Princess Aurora in *Sleeping Beauty*, its tulle still stiff despite hours of use, and the peasant costume for *Coppélia*, red and green with a laced bodice and frothy white skirt. The costumes, she knew, looked better on stage than on the racks, where their magic disappeared, their glitter only

sequins, their fabric worn and the stains of sweat and
stage make-up visible on the seams.

As the girl in Gregory's ballet, Carrie was to wear a
pale yellow costume with a long skirt that had once
adorned her when she was a flower in *The Nutcracker*.
Since it had been made for her only two years ago, Mrs.
Martinelli had left the fitting for the last minute, assum-
ing as Carrie did that the costume would fit perfectly, but
now she was fussing and muttering, her mouth full of
pins, her head shaking as Carrie stood before her.

'What's the matter?' Carrie asked.

'It's no good. Not in the bodice and waist.'

Carrie felt the bones in the bodice pinching under her
arms, and frowned at her slender image in the mirror.
'But I haven't put on any weight. I'm hardly eating—in
fact, I've lost a few pounds.'

Mrs Martinelli pursed her lips. 'I'll have to add
another row of hooks.'

'But that's impossible!' Carrie looked at her with
dismay. She had thought she was doing so well. Was
Bonnie's scale off? Casimir hadn't said anything—but
then his mind was rarely off his latest conquest, and
when she thought about it, they had hardly rehearsed
together during the past two weeks.

'Not impossible,' Mrs Martinelli said, standing up.
'You've gained here and here.' She patted her own
plump breasts and belly. 'It reminds me of when I was
pregnant with Joey, but then I know you dancers are too
careful for that.'

She turned to get her marking chalk, while Carrie
stared at her reflection, her eyes widening, a sudden
understanding causing them to darken. The irregularity
of her system which was caused, one doctor had told her,
by dieting and heavy exertion, had lulled her into a
foolish complacency. What an idiot she was! she thought
with despair. The evidence had been before her for
weeks; the exhaustion and nausea all adding up to one

horrifying fact. She had become pregnant in Naples; she was carrying Alex Taylor's baby!

'Now, hold still while I mark this,' Mrs Martinelli was saying, but Carrie barely heard her.

She was remembering those nights of love. No, of sex, she reminded herself with a harsh brutality. Of course, Alex hadn't said anything about the possibility of a pregnancy. He had assumed that any woman of Carrie's obvious sophistication would be quite capable of taking care of the problem herself. The trouble was that Carrie was far from being so knowledgeable, and in fact the idea that she could get pregnant had never once crossed her mind. She associated babies with a husband and family, not with a casual affair conducted under the Florida moonlight.

Pregnant. She said the word to herself over and over again as if she could dull it by repetition, but nothing could blunt its meaning. Pregnant meant that she would bear a child and be a mother. Pregnant meant that she wouldn't be able to dance for much longer. *Babies ruin bodies*, Gregory had said. Would hers be ruined? Would that body she relied on for its strength and flexibility be lost to her? Carrie closed her eyes so that she could no longer see her reflection. The slim woman in the mirror was merely an illusion; the woman within had altered irrevocably. She had crossed an invisible line, and there was no going back, no retreat possible. She knew that she had the choice of abortion, but she also knew that for her it was no choice at all. She had participated in the creation of a new life, and, for her, that child, tiny, soft and helpless, was already precious and loved.

CHAPTER THREE

CARRIE stood on the patio of her parents' home in Marin County and looked down at the breathtaking view of San Francisco, its buildings white under the hot afternoon sun. Below her the hills leading down to the bay were lush and green, and the water sparkled blue. The sky was clear and brilliant, only one small fluffy cloud marring its purity. In the distance she could see the beginning of the Pacific Ocean, its entrance marked by the Golden Gate Bridge, a gleaming network of girders and wires. Although she was too far away to catch the scent of the ocean, she remembered how its salty mist could spread over the city like a light blanket.

She sighed deeply and then turned to walk back into the living room, where she was assailed by a pang of nostalgia so pervasive that it made her take a shuddering breath. Every ornament and piece of furniture held a memory for her; the rocker she used to sit on as a little girl when weariness made her head droop, a crewel-work cushion that she'd watched her mother work on for hours, a nautical lamp she had bought for her father one Christmas. Carrie remembered her childhood as pleasant and uncomplicated; hours of playing in the shaded yard and riding her bicycle down the suburban streets. Her father was a corporate lawyer, her mother dabbled in art, and they had given her everything she had ever wanted and needed in addition to the comfort and stability of a living home.

When she thought what her news would do to them, now fully confirmed by her doctor, Carrie felt a chasm of fear and unhappiness widen within her. They would be devastated, she knew that. They took such pride and pleasure in her career, often shaking their heads in admiration at her drive and skill. When they learned that she had become pregnant by a man she barely knew, they would be hurt beyond belief. Look at them now, she thought with sadness, as she watched her family all gathered around the coffee table, going through the photo album and scrapbook, laughing over their recollections. With one word she could ruin the day, shattering their happiness the way a stone breaks glass, leaving it in brittle, pointed shards.

'Carrie,' her sister Julie said with a smile, 'come and see this one of you at six months bawling your head off!'

Carrie slowly walked around to the couch and looked over Julie's shoulder at the photograph of herself as a baby. Was that what her baby would look like? Would it resemble her, or would it take after Alex? She shivered inside at the thought of a small boy with his father's dark hair and eyes.

'I think there's a resemblance between Ryan and Carrie when she was a baby,' said Elizabeth Moore. 'A definite resemblance. Look at the eyes.'

Julie's husband, David, put on a look of dismay. 'And here I thought my son took after me!'

Joshua Moore patted his son-in-law on the shoulder. 'All babies look alike,' he said. 'I can't even tell Julie or Carrie's baby pictures apart.'

Julie gave him a mock-reproachful look. 'And I always thought I was the beautiful one!'

'You were both beautiful,' he said genially. 'I had two beautiful daughters.'

Julie leaned over and gave him a kiss. 'You old diplomatl!' she smiled.

Listening to them brought a lump to Carrie's throat. She loved them all and they trusted her so completely. What would her tall, distinguished father say when she broke the news? Or her mother, Elizabeth; short, brown-haired and chock full of energy, who had spent hours driving Carrie to ballet lessons and sewing costumes? And then there was Julie, who could have been Carrie's twin. They were only two years apart and they both had the same slender frame, hair colour and a similar face shape. What would she think of the way her sister had behaved? Would she condemn her for a momentary loss of restraint and sheer stupidity?

It was odd, Carrie reflected, that she was the one caught in a mess when Julie had always been the trouble-maker. Carrie had been quiet and peaceful; Julie had been bouncy and noisy, a mischievous hell-raiser who accepted punishment stoically and then went on to commit the next crime. To everyone's surprise she had fallen in love and married a man of whom the whole family approved. David was an attractive, blond six-footer who worked for a highly successful firm of architects. Their son, Ryan, had been born after two years of an apparently happy marriage and was already, Julie insisted, spoiled rotten by his grandparents.

'The kid has so many toys,' she said to Carrie later as they helped wash up the dinner dishes, 'that there's no room in his crib to sleep.'

'He's a darling,' said Carrie.

Julie gave her a happy smile. 'Spoken like a devoted aunt!'

What else could Carrie say? She was utterly fascinated with Julie's baby and had already watched him for hours. He was adorable, a fat little cherub with big blue eyes like Julie's and a few wisps of fair hair. He gurgled, smiled and waved his fists in the air. She had seen Julie feeding him and wondered how she would feel, holding such a morsel of humanity in her arms, a small mouth tugging at her breast.

'The premiere is tomorrow,' Julie was saying. 'Are you nervous?'

Carrie wiped a saucepan and put it in the cupboard. 'A bit,' she confessed. 'But then I always feel like I'm hosting a butterfly conference before a performance.'

Elizabeth came in, carrying a casserole, and smiled at Carrie. 'You'll do well. You always do.'

Carrie gave Julie a rueful grin. 'Let's just hope the critics listen to Mom!'

Elizabeth was unperturbed. 'They'll recognise genius when they see it,' she said as Carrie groaned.

'Which reminds me, Carrie,' said Julie, 'I think I was mistaken for you a couple of weeks ago. I was downtown shopping, pushing Ryan in his stroller, when a man came up behind me and put his hand on my shoulder. I turned around and I don't know who was more shocked, him or me. I thought I was about to be attacked, and he looked as if he'd seen a ghost.'

'Maybe you just have one of those common faces,' Carrie teased.

'No,' said Julie, her voice serious. 'He didn't call me by your name, but I'm sure he thought I was you. He just stared at me, muttered something about my hair being the same and then apologised profusely. I was wearing my hair down that day.'

A premonition, Carrie discovered, can have the same stunning force as an unwanted truth. 'Oh,' was all she managed to say.

Julie took the shock that paled her sister's cheeks as a sign of romantic intrigue. 'He was tall,' she said with a grin, 'dark and absolutely gorgeous. Know anyone like that?'

Carrie cleared her throat and tried to sound nonchalant. 'No,' she said.

'Oh, Mom,' said Julie, turning to Elizabeth who was emerging from a rearrangement of the refrigerator, 'I think Carrie's been hiding something from us.'

'Hiding what?'

'A boy-friend.'

Elizabeth turned to Carrie with interest. 'Carrie, you never said . . .'

'It's all in Julie's imagination,' Carrie rushed to protest, throwing an angry look in Julie's direction.

Julie was undaunted. 'You're blushing,' she teased.

Determined to squelch any further insinuation, Carrie said forcefully, 'I have no boy-friends.'

Elizabeth put her arm around her and shook her head warningly at Julie. 'I'm sure,' she said comfortingly, 'that you'll tell us all about it when you're ready, but I just want you to know that your father and I aren't worried about the choice you make. We know you'll pick the right man.'

'Like me,' Julie said gaily.

Elizabeth gave her a dry but affectionate look. 'In your case, I think we had the benefit of good luck.'

Julie winked at Carrie. 'She still can't believe that I had the good taste to marry David.'

'You have to admit,' said Elizabeth, 'that you went out with some of the most unsuitable young men. Beads, fringes, long hair and guitars—that was Julie's idea of eligible. David was a welcome relief.'

Julie picked up another dish towel. 'And you think Carrie will be any better?'

'I could always trust Carrie,' said Elizabeth, giving her a final squeeze before heading back into the dining room. 'She's always sensible.'

Carrie dressed for the opening of Gregory's ballet in a sombre, depressed mood. She wanted to tell her parents about her pregnancy during her stay with them, but she just couldn't bear to burst that bubble of confidence that they had in her. Her parents doted on baby Ryan, but how would they feel about a grandchild whose very existence would point to their daughter's shame? Carrie knew that nothing she did could be hidden. The press would pick up any rumour with alacrity, and the gossip-mongers would be searching for clues to the father's identity. Her past would be up for scrutiny and every man she had ever dated or looked at twice would be seen as a candidate. Casimir would, of course, be the most likely choice. He would love it, Carrie thought with a touch of irony. He loved any proof of his masculine charisma.

'Ready, Miss Moore?'

Carrie nodded to the stagehand as she tied a knot in the ribbon of her yellow pointe shoes and gave herself one last glance in the mirror. She looked young enough to be the adolescent girl of the ballet. Her hair, pulled back and held under a cap of net and sequins, left her slender face looking very vulnerable, the heavy stage make-up accenting the slant of her eyes and the hollows of her cheeks. The yellow costume bared her shoulders and arms; its chiffon skirt allowed glimpses of her long, slender legs. Later, when she danced the love scene with Casimir, her hair would be loosened to hang down her back, giving her a wild, uncontrolled look, but at the beginning she was to appear pure and chaste, untouched by any man.

Carrie danced that night as she had never danced before, fuelled by the fear that this ballet would be her last. She danced for the girl she had once been and for her parents in the audience whose trust in her would be so cruelly broken. She danced before Casimir with a seductiveness that was underlaid by the knowledge of the child within her, its curled presence giving meaning to the act of love. She was passionate, tender, hurt and bewildered. All the emotions that had buffeted her since her stay in Naples were reflected in the lyrical move-ments of her body. It had always been like this for her: dancing was the only way Carrie could express what lay in her heart.

At the end of it all, she was alone on the stage, roses in her arms, in a deep curtsey before a wild, cheering audience. She could see nothing but tiers upon tiers of blurred faces beyond the stage lights, but the roar of the crowd crashed over her like a tidal wave. She straightened up and curtsied again, humbled and overwhelmed by her ability to create this adoration. It was always this moment that frightened Carrie most, and the knowledge that she was the magnet that drew those eyes and cheers. Success weighed on her as an awesome burden. She felt that each performance was a responsibility and that failure lurked before every step. One bad night would disappoint her audience, and the critics would tear her apart like predatory cats.

'Bravo!' the audience cried, and Carrie took one final bow, her eyes glancing upwards to the box where her parents were seated. She could see their happy faces; her father was making a victory sign with his fingers. She smiled slightly to herself—and then, looking down at the next box, froze in place. A man stood in the box just below them, a man with black hair and broad shoulders and a face that had been etched on her memory for all time. For a second, Carrie thought she would never be able to move again, but she recovered, took another dipping curtsey and then ran, trembling, off stage to the congratulations of Gregory.

'Darling, you were magnificent! Magnificent!' he exclaimed, throwing his arms around her. 'They loved you, they loved the ballet!'

There were others who joined him in the large company dressing room to shower her with praise. Her parents arrived, their faces glowing with pride, and Julie and David gave her big hugs. Casimir called her his *milaya*, beloved, and bestowed upon her a spray of roses. The room began to look like a hothouse and the scent of opened blossoms permeated the air. Glasses clinked, voices and laughter filled the air, and champagne flowed. In the midst of it, Carrie stood like an automated doll, her smile permanently affixed, nodding to those who spoke to her and murmuring thanks. Every time the door opened, her startled eyes would glance at the entrance to see who had arrived, her heart lurching in anticipation, but when Alex did come, she had turned away to talk to a well-wisher and had no idea that he had arrived.

It was Julie who got to her first. 'He's here!' she exclaimed in excitement.

·Carrie looked at her in bewilderment. 'Who's here?'

'The man I told you about; the one who thought I was you.'

Carrie held herself rigid, forced herself not to turn around. 'Really?' she asked.

Julie took one glance at Carrie's expression and a mischievous glint came into her eyes. 'He's coming this way,' she said, looking beyond Carrie's shoulder.

Carrie finally crumpled under the tension. 'Alone?' she asked breathlessly, her heart pounding in great, heavy beats.

'Yes . . . no, wait a minute. Oops, I think a woman came in with him.'

Carrie stiffened her back. 'Oh?'

Julie threw her a disappointed look. 'And you can bet your bottom dollar it isn't his mother.'

'I told you,' Carrie whispered urgently, 'he isn't my boy-friend.'

'I know what you told me, but . . .' Julie stopped abruptly and turned to someone with a gracious smile. 'I'll bet you're here to see the star,' she said as Carrie slowly swivelled around, her hands trembling and moist.

Alex stood before her in a dark suit whose well-tailored lines moulded his muscles into a lean sophistication. His face was every bit as handsome as she remembered. How could she have forgotten the perfection of his mouth or the dark eyes under their wide-set black brows? For a second he appraised her, still dressed in her yellow costume, her honey-brown hair hanging down her back, and then his glance flicked to Julie and he gave a grim smile.

Julie rose to the occasion. 'We've met, haven't we?' she asked brightly.

'I believe so.'

'You must have thought I was Carrie,' she said with a small, tentative laugh.

'It did cross my mind,' he said drily.

Julie cleared her throat as she glanced at Carrie's pale face. 'Well, I'm sure you two have some private things to discuss. I'll go find David.'

'There's no need,' said Carrie, grabbing for her arm, but Julie quickly disappeared into the crowd. She took a deep breath and faced Alex.

'The elusive Bonnie Hughes,' he said in a low voice.

'It's . . . nice to see you again,' she said politely, hoping that her voice wouldn't waver and reveal what she was feeling. Although she hadn't forgotten what Alex looked like, she discovered that memory had dulled the impact of his masculine sensuality. She hadn't remembered the force it had on her or the way his look could make her legs go weak.

'Is Caroline Moore a stage name?' he asked.

Carrie shook her head. 'It's my real name.'

'You just use Bonnie for vacations?'

Carrie looked down at the floor. 'I'd never done anything like that before,' she confessed.

'I bet,' he said curtly.

'Really,' she protested, 'I . . .'

'Alex darling, I lost you in the crowd.' The woman who had come up to them put her arm through Alex's and gave Carrie a glittering smile. 'You were wonderful, Miss Moore. Wonderful!'

'Thank you,' Carrie said politely, while she took in the other woman's extraordinary beauty. She had auburn hair that hung in a thick curtain to her shoulders, lovely green eyes and a flawless complexion. Her evening dress was a shimmering gold, low-cut and seductive, clinging as it did to her voluptuous curves.

'This is Leona Sole,' said Alex, and Carrie sucked in her breath. Everyone in San Francisco knew about the Soles; they owned half of the downtown real estate. Leona's picture frequently adorned the gossip columns of the papers and her parties were known for their extravagant opulence. She shouldn't have been surprised, Carrie thought dismally, to find Alex in such elevated company. Not with his good looks and contacts.

'Oh,' said Leona, looking from Alex to Carrie and back, her green eyes watchful. 'Do you two know one another?'

'We've met before,' said Alex.

'I had to drag him here,' Leona confided to Carrie. 'Believe it or not, the man had never been to a ballet before! And he liked it, didn't you, darling?' She leaned closer to him, turning her face up to his.

Alex didn't look at the woman hanging on his arm but down at Carrie. 'You made it come alive for me, Miss Moore,' he said with a politeness that she knew was only a thin veneer for mockery.

Carrie couldn't restrain the devilish impulse that leapt up within her. 'You learn something new every day,' she said, lifting her chin and daring him with her eyes. 'Don't you?'

She slept until ten the next morning, awakening to find the sun streaming through the curtains, its rays illuminating the cracked and worn faces on a row of dolls she had collected as a child. Her mother was a hoarder; she never threw anything away, and Carrie was always amused to find that her bedroom looked much the way she had left it eight years before when she had set off for New York, decorated in pink and white dotted Swiss cotton with a canopy bed and a plush white carpet.

She stretched and then sat up, tucking her knees

under her chin, the hem of her white nightgown touching her toes. She deliberately stared at her childhood toys, trying not to think of the evening before, but she knew it was hopeless. The braid of her hair fell over one shoulder and she wrapped its end around one finger, her eyes pensive. Seeing Alex had disturbed her far more than she liked to admit. She knew that she was still attracted to him and she felt a poignant irony that the father of her unborn child had seen her and not known about the life she was carrying within her, the one he had helped create. Not that she could tell him, she mused. He might interfere and try to take control of her. He was that type of man. You could sense the power and mastery in him; he wouldn't take the news of a child lightly.

Alex was angry with her. Their conversation the night before had been interrupted by Leona and then another well-wisher, but Carrie had felt his eyes on her and sensed his baffled fury. She had given him the brush-off in Florida and then rubbed his nose in it. He had shown remarkable restraint, she supposed, in not throttling her when he had the chance. She knew that she had acted abominably. She sighed and pressed her forehead to her knees, unwilling to admit, even to herself, that she had had another motive for taking a cut at Alex's ego. She didn't like to think that their affair in Florida had just been a short, romantic interlude for him. She hated the thought that other women had provided him with that kind of pleasure before and would do so again. He could count her as a conquest, but he was the first man she had ever known. For her the earth had shaken and tilted on its axis, nothing would be the same again.

'Carrie? Are you up, dear?' Elizabeth's voice came up the stairs and Carrie lifted her head.

'Yes.'

'I've made you some breakfast.'

'Thanks, Mom, I'll be right down.'

She shared a quiet breakfast with her mother and then

took a shower. Her father had gone to work earlier and Elizabeth had planned a morning of work in the front garden. Carrie looked forward to a restful day. Perhaps she would see a few of her old friends; several had said they might stop by. She sat out on the patio, letting her long fall of honey-brown hair dry in the sun. There was a hint of fall in the air, but the day promised to be hot in the afternoon and Carrie was dressed in a pair of white shorts and a halter top. She leaned back in the chaise-longue and closed her eyes, letting the sun make yellow swirls on her eyelids. She deliberately pushed away her problems and relaxed, putting her mind into neutral and listening to the sounds of birds in the trees and the hum of a lawnmower in the distance.

She heard a step behind her and called out, 'Mom, come on and enjoy the sun. It's beautiful!'

'I agree.'

The deep baritone caused her eyes to fly open, and she looked up to see Alex standing beside her.

She sat up abruptly, her hair tumbling down her bared back. 'How did you get in?' she asked breathlessly.

'Your mother was very hospitable. She let me in through the front door.' Alex sat down on a chair, his lean body in its brown slacks and cream silk shirt looking carelessly elegant, his black hair gleaming obsidian in the sun.

Carrie's heart had begun that pounding, uncomfortable rhythm. She desperately wanted him to go away and leave her alone. She didn't like the way his dark gaze was running up the long, naked length of her legs to rest on the skimpy covering of her halter top. 'If you've come to see me, I'm afraid . . .'

'We have to talk.'

'We have nothing to talk about.'

'I don't like being conned,' he said, and his lazy posture did not fool Carrie. Anger made the muscles in his jaw clench and hardened his strong features.

Fright made her voice shake slightly. 'I didn't mean to con you.'

'Weren't you lucky that I'd been out of the country for a year? Otherwise I might have recognised you in Florida.'

Carrie let her dark lashes shade the humiliated look in her eyes. 'You might have,' she agreed in a low voice.

'I wonder what I would have done,' he said gratingly, 'if I had? Were you afraid that I'd take you to bed just for the glamour of making love to a celebrity?'

'Alex, please,' she begged, turning to see if her mother was coming. Elizabeth was a good hostess; Carrie guessed that she was preparing a tray of drinks and snacks for their guest.

'Or were you merely having a little bit of fun at my expense?' he asked, his voice bitter.

Carrie flushed. 'You seemed to enjoy it,' she flared at him.

'It wasn't mutual?' One black eyebrow arched sardonically.

She looked away. 'I don't want to talk about it any more.'

'Brave in public,' Alex said sarcastically, 'and a coward in private.'

The opening of the glass door of the patio ended their exchange, and Carrie breathed a sigh of relief at her mother's arrival. Alex was right; she felt far safer when she wasn't alone with him. She was afraid of what he would say and do; he had a power to wound her that made her body tense in his presence, constantly aware of the baby within her and that everything she said was a lie and a sham.

'I hope you like lemonade, Mr Taylor,' Elizabeth said gaily. 'I thought it might be too warm for coffee.'

Alex stood up and gallantly took the tray from her hands. 'I'm very fond of lemonade, Mrs Moore.'

Over drinks and slices of cake, Alex and Elizabeth chatted like old friends about the weather, the latest political crisis and the recent bus strike, while Carrie fumed at the ease with which he charmed her mother. She noticed that Elizabeth had changed from her gardening denims into a pair of pale green slacks and a matching top. It was not lost on her that most women were susceptible to an attractive male like Alex, but she had rather hoped that her mother would prove immune. Carrie didn't want Elizabeth to approve of Alex; she needed an ally in this battle against a man who seemed intent upon cutting her down to size.

'And how did you and Carrie meet?' her mother was saying brightly, and Carrie's head shot up from the contemplation of her entwined fingers.

'In Florida, Mrs Moore. We were both on holiday.'

'I didn't know you'd gone to Florida, dear.'

'It was just a short trip. Nothing exciting.' Carrie threw a warning look at Alex and he gave her a small, mirthless grin.

'Did you go with Bonnie?'

Carrie swallowed. 'No, she was working.'

Alex's tone was casual as he helped himself to another piece of cake. 'Who is Bonnie?'

'Carrie and Bonnie share an apartment in New York,' Elizabeth explained. 'More lemonade, Mr Taylor?'

'Please, call me Alex,' he said, holding out his glass.

Elizabeth beamed at him as she poured the lemonade from its pitcher. 'It's so nice to see Carrie getting out more. Her father and I have often thought that her career has taken a severe toll on her social life. Our other daughter is married already and has a baby.'

Carrie looked at her mother in astonishment. Her parents had never mentioned being unhappy with her life as a dancer, and it had not occurred to her that they wanted the same things for her as they did for Julie. She had always assumed that they approved of her goal to be a prima ballerina, even though it might mean that she would never marry and have children.

'Your daughter is too pretty, Mrs Moore, to lead a solitary life.'

Carrie glared at Alex and wished she could wring his neck. He was far too smooth and dangerous.

Elizabeth had no such qualms. 'That's what we keep telling ourselves,' she said with a smile.

Carrie didn't like being talked about as if she weren't there. 'I like the way I live.'

Elizabeth patted her hand. 'Of course you do, dear. You haven't tried anything else.' She turned to Alex. 'Do you live here in San Francisco?'

'I keep an apartment here,' Alex told her, 'but I also have one in New York and one in Houston.'

Carrie's heart sank as Elizabeth asked Alex questions about his work. It was one thing to meet Alex in San Francisco, knowing that soon she would leave and the geographical distance between them would provide an ample barrier of protection, but it was quite another to realise that he lived part of the time in Manhattan. For all she knew, his apartment might be right around the corner from hers. New York was like that. It was so large and so populous that it was quite conceivable that two neighbours in the same apartment building could be strangers. She and Alex might have passed within hailing distance of one another several times in the past few months and never known it.

'. . . and I had the afternoon off,' Alex was saying, 'and I thought I might take Carrie to lunch.'

'What a nice idea!' Elizabeth gave her daughter an encouraging smile. 'Don't you think so, dear?'

Carrie saw that it was going to be impossible to turn down Alex's invitation. Her mother knew that she had nothing planned, and if there was one thing Elizabeth was a stickler for it was good manners. 'It sounds charming,' she agreed reluctantly.

'Why don't you run up and change while I keep Alex company for you?'

Carrie caught the amused glint in Alex's eyes as she stood up and stiffened her spine in anger. She stalked into the house and up into her bedroom, where she brushed her hair until it sparked and then slipped on a pale lemon sundress and a pair of straw espadrilles. Her conduct during lunch, she decided with cool fury, was going to turn Alex off. Not that he would be able to fault her. Carrie knew just the right tone to take—uninterested and indifferent. She was going to make damn sure that Alex Taylor never wanted to see her again!

Alex took her to a small restaurant in Chinatown which was up a narrow flight of stairs and was decorated in red and black with gold dragons curling ferociously on the chairs and walls. They had a table right by the window and Carrie could watch the hustle and bustle of Grant Avenue, one of San Francisco's most famous streets. The area hummed with activity. Crowds of tourists walked up and down the sidewalks, staring into the windows of stores that sold hundreds of oriental items; paper fans, red and black lacquered bowls, jade and ivory jewellery, wildly coloured paper kites. The traffic was never-ending and small slant-eyed children darted in and out between the cars and the passersby. Carrie discovered that she'd quite forgotten how exciting and exotic Chinatown was.

'Is it that fascinating?'

Carrie turned from the window. 'I haven't been here in a long time.'

'You don't come home very often?'

'Not as much as I would like.'

The waiter interrupted them and took their order, while Carrie surreptitiously watched Alex's handsome profile. She wondered why he was taking her out to lunch. His only motive could be revenge, and surely the best revenge was to ignore her. If she were Alex, she would be taking great pains to make sure that their paths never crossed again. There were other women in his life; that she knew, and he didn't strike her as the kind of man who hung around celebrities. That type was instantaneously recognisable; they fawned and flattered, more interested in who Carrie was than what she was like.

'You're frowning,' Alex observed as the waiter left.

Carrie decided to take the matter into her hands. 'I'm wondering why we're here.'

'You don't know?' The voice was mocking.

'No,' she said curtly.

He leaned forward over the white damask table. 'I find it hard to believe that what happened in Florida could leave you so cold.'

'Maybe I've done it before,' she said with a shrug.

'That's a damned lie. We both know that.'

Carrie coloured slightly at his reference to her previous state of innocence. 'Maybe I have other, more important, things to think about.'

Alex sat back, his dark eyes watchful. 'I just can't equate you with the woman who danced last night. She had a warm sensuality; she wasn't hard and cold.'

'That was a part,' Carrie pointed out. 'It was a fictitious role.'

'Are you saying that anyone could have danced it with that emotional intensity?'

'I'm an artist,' she said. 'It's my job to imagine that I'm someone else, a different person with another personality than my own.'

Their meal arrived, and Carrie was thankful for the interruption. Alex was far too perceptive. She sipped at the steaming liquid of her won-ton soup, and was glad he couldn't see her face. She didn't want him poking and prying into the way she had danced the night before. She knew that she had danced with her heart on her sleeve,

and that anyone with insight would recognise the rawness of the feelings she had exposed. Would she have
been different if she had known that Alex was in the
audience? Carrie wasn't sure; when she danced, she
forgot about the world around her and all that existed
was the stage and the movements of her body.

'So you don't have much of a social life?'

She wished Elizabeth hadn't been so frank. 'My
mother doesn't know what I do,' she said guardedly.

Alex gave a small smile. 'I've always wondered about
those male dancers.'

'They're not as effeminate as you may imagine,' Carrie said heatedly. She knew how the public viewed male
ballet dancers and it made her angry. They were a
diverse group with an assortment of interests and personalities. The fact that they made a career of dancing did
not necessarily mean that they were abnormal in any
way. And physically, they were superb specimens. An
evening's performance was the equivalent of a vigorous
ten-mile run.

'What about the man you were dancing with?'

'Casimir?' She gave an unconscious sigh. 'Believe me,
he's all man!'

Alex had noted her sigh and gave it another interpretation. 'You go out with him?'

The question was asked casually, but Carrie thought
she detected something beneath his indifference and she
saw her chance. If Alex believed that she was involved in
some way with Casimir, it might dampen whatever
interest he had in her.

She looked down as if she were embarrassed to discuss
her love life. 'Yes.'

'But the relationship isn't too serious,' he said calmly.

Carrie glanced at him. 'Why do you say that?'

Alex shrugged, his mouth in a knowing smile. 'Because you haven't slept with him.'

His arrogant belief that he had her pegged and

classified made her furious. 'Not before I met you,' she agreed coldly. 'But things have changed.'

'Have they?' His dark eyes were hard.

This was going to be the hardest lie of all. She could feel part of her resisting the words that rose to her lips, blocking them from being uttered. By nature she was a truthful person, who believed that honesty was important. She wasn't accustomed to the type of double-dealing that talking with Alex required. Still, she had to say it because the confession, she knew, would protect her from Alex himself. 'Yes,' she said, raising her amber eyes to his and giving him the full benefit of their golden clarity, 'they have.'

CHAPTER FOUR

BONNIE was the first person to notice that Carrie was pregnant. She had come back from her European vacation during the ballet's tour in San Francisco, and Carrie returned home to find her tanned and full of stories about French men. She also had brought home several suitcases of new clothes, increasing an already voluminous wardrobe, and Carrie couldn't help teasing her about the state of her closets.

'Don't you ever get rid of anything?' she asked during one lazy Saturday afternoon, as she lay back on the bed in Bonnie's room and watched her search through a crowded closet for a dress she was planning to wear to a party that night.

'Never. I develop an attachment that can last a lifetime.' Bonnie rummaged through the hangers and then groaned when one dress fell off and landed in a heap on a pile of shoes.

'You'd be far better off developing attachments to people.'

'If you're talking about men, then let me tell you that clothes are far more reliable. They can't walk out and they don't talk back.' Bonnie spoke from the depths of a walk-in closet that was lined in cedar. Her bedroom was one of the most lavishly designed rooms in the apartment. It was decorated all in shades of red and white, from the thick ivory carpet to the scarlet fringe on a lampshade. She had a queen-size bed, a divan, a makeup table and several lounging chairs in red velvet.

'Do I detect a note of bitterness?' Carrie asked.

Bonnie emerged from the closet, triumphantly carrying three dresses. 'Bitterness? No, it's just a fact of life, and since I believe in the old biblical adage about an eye for an eye, I simply pay them back in kind. You should have seen the look on Pierre's face when I showed up at the casino with Jean-Paul!'

Carrie had already heard the complicated story of Bonnie's romantic adventures in Nice. She had had two affairs going at the same time, juggling men with a consummate skill that required an unbelievable amount of nerve and confidence. Bonnie seemed to have enjoyed herself, but Carrie was of the opinion that if she tried the same manoeuvres, the stress alone would do her in.

She propped herself up on one elbow. 'You're lucky that duelling is outlawed!'

Bonnie shrugged nonchalantly at the thought of two men fighting to the death over her. 'Men's egos are outsized to begin with. No harm done in cutting them down to size and having a little fun at the same time.'

Carrie watched her lay the three dresses across the divan and regard them with a frown. Although she admired Bonnie's carefree attitude towards men, Carrie had always wondered what lay behind that flippancy. Her shortlived marriage had been a mismatch that both partners had been eager to terminate, and Bonnie had never hinted at any acrimony or battles. Still, she had a cynicism about men that hinted at something that went far beyond the simple divorce that Carrie envisioned. Perhaps, she thought, Bonnie had gone into her almost prearranged marriage with far greater expectations and hopes than she had ever revealed.

Bonnie held one dress, a slinky number in mauve chiffon, up to her bathrobe-clad body and stared into the mirror, tilting her blonde head to one side in an appraising fashion. 'What do you think?'

'I've always liked that dress.'

Bonnie grimaced. 'The colour makes me look like a corpse.'

'Oh, I don't think so!' Carrie said in surprise. Bonnie had worn the dress to last year's Christmas party for the Manhattan Ballet, and Carrie had thought that she looked lovely, the soft purple setting off her golden hair and deepening the blue of her eyes.

Bonnie took another glance into the mirror and shook her head. 'You can have it. It was always a little too small on me anyway.' They were close to the same size; Bonnie's figure was fuller, Carrie was slightly shorter.

'But . . .'

'No buts.' Bonnie shook her head with determination. 'Try it on.'

'I don't need . . .'

Bonnie narrowed her eyes and sized Carrie up. 'The colour is perfect; it will set off your eyes. I always like gold and mauve together.' She put the dress on the bed before Carrie, who sat up with a sigh. She had never had any luck fighting off Bonnie's generosity and, as a result, has a closetful of magnificent dresses and outfits that Bonnie no longer wanted. Besides, Carrie knew that if she didn't take the dress, it would be shipped off to a charity the next day.

She slipped out of her bathrobe and pulled the dress over her head as Bonnie turned a judgmental look on the second dress on the divan. 'Zip me up, will you?' Carrie asked, turning her back.

Bonnie obliged, or tried to oblige, until it became obvious that the dress was too tight across Carrie's hips. 'This should fit you,' she said with a frown.

Carrie tried desperately to act as if it were nothing. She hadn't had any trouble with her clothes yet, only the tight-fitting costume for Gregory's ballet had required alteration, but she knew that a subtle thickening of her waistline and rib cage had taken place. She hadn't thought it would be noticeable, but the mauve dress with its silken underskirt was designed to fit like a second skin and had no room for camouflage.

'I gained a bit of weight on tour,' she said with nonchalance. 'You know my mother's cooking.'

Bonnie walked around in front of her and stared at Carrie. 'I could have sworn that you're thinner than you used to be. At least your face is.' She looked down at the offending waistline and then back up again, an expression of disbelief swiftly passing over her face. 'Carrie, you couldn't be . . .'

'I'm not . . . it's only . . .' Carrie stammered, trying to deny the truth, but the words wouldn't come. How long could she keep her pregnancy secret from Bonnie anyway? Her room-mate was far too perceptive and knowing, and Carrie was already a bit surprised that Bonnie hadn't seen through the charade of cheerful good humour that she had been playing since her return from San Francisco. Now, the expression on her face confirmed Bonnie's fears, and Carrie simply felt relief that the whole farce was over; she knew that she couldn't have kept it up much longer.

'You're pregnant!' Bonnie exclaimed in a horrified whisper.

Carrie nodded, then put her trembling hands up to her face at Bonnie's sudden look of compassion. So far she had borne the burden of her pregnancy with an unyielding stoicism, forcing herself not to think about it or, when she did, to bite her lip and face it head on, but Bonnie's shock and sympathy undermined the wall she had built around herself, and to her utter mortification, she began to cry.

'Carrie!' Bonnie pulled her over to the bed and, sitting down with her, put her arm around Carrie's shoulders. 'Baby, is it Casimir?'

The thought of Casimir fathering her baby was so ludicrous that it forced Carrie to lift her head and give Bonnie a tremulous smile. 'God forbid!' she exclaimed.

'If it isn't Casimir, then who is it?' Bonnie asked in bafflement. 'You never go out on dates, you never go anywhere, you're the most domesticated . . .' She suddenly stopped. 'My God, it's that man in Florida!' She threw Carrie a sudden glance. 'It is, isn't it?'

Carrie nodded and squeezed her eyes shut to hold back the tears.

Bonnie held Carrie tightly. 'Oh, baby, haven't you ever heard of birth control?'

'I didn't expect . . . I never thought . . .' The words came out in muffled, shaky snatches. 'Oh, Bonnie, I was so stupid!'

But Bonnie wasn't interested in mutual accusation; she was too busy counting. 'You're almost four months pregnant. Is that too late for an abortion?'

Carrie shook her head violently from side to side. 'I don't want an abortion.'

Bonnie was silent for a second. 'Have you told Gregory?'

'No.'

'This ends your dancing for the season.'

'I . . . know.'

For minutes Bonnie simply held on to Carrie, letting her cry, stroking her hair and rubbing her back where the unzipped bodice of the mauve dress exposed her skin. Carrie indulged in every feeling of despair that had overwhelmed her during the past weeks and, like a dam breaking loose, the tears seemed to flow in an endless stream. She found a surprising comfort in Bonnie's arms, in the soothing murmurs of her voice and the warm hand on her back. For a brief time she felt like a child again, protected and safe from the world, pushing away the knowledge that she would have to face reality soon enough.

'What about the father?' Bonnie asked when Carrie's sobs subsided and the room was quiet.

Carrie straightened up and blew her nose on a tissue. 'What about him?'

'Does he know?'

'Of course not!'

'Are you going to tell him?'

'No.' Carrie hadn't heard from Alex again after that very awkward lunch in San Francisco and could only assume that her supposed love affair with Casimir had discouraged him. As Bonnie had said, men had large egos, and it was quite obvious that Alex couldn't handle any suggestion that she had gone from his arms into those of another man.

'Don't you think he has a right to know?'

Carrie shook her head vehemently.

'What if he looks you up and notices that you're pregnant?' Bonnie asked patiently.

'I used your name.'

'What!'

Carrie cleared her throat and gave Bonnie a shamed look. 'I lied about who I was and used your maiden name. I told him I worked in advertising.'

Bonnie looked at her in amazement.

'I didn't want him to know about me or what I was,' Carrie stammered. 'I wanted to be . . . someone different for a change.'

'No wonder you got pregnant,' Bonnie said drily, her blue eyes knowing. 'In a fantasy world you don't have to worry about mundane things like babies.'

Carrie sighed. 'It's none of his business anyway.'

'It'll be his child, too,' Bonnie pointed out.

Carrie sat up straighter. 'It was a fling for him, Bonnie, a short weekend affair with no strings attached. That's the way he wanted it and that's the way I wanted it. It's over, done with, the end.'

Bonnie laid a gentle hand on Carrie's wrist. 'But it isn't over. There's another life to contend with . . .'

Carrie stood up, albeit shakily but with determination. 'The baby is my responsibility, not his.'

Her friend took one glance at the set line of her mouth

and capitulated. 'Okay, if you don't want the father to know . . .'

'I don't,' Carrie said firmly.

'Then,' said Bonnie with a slight sigh, 'we'll just have to manage without him.'

The fact that Bonnie knew about the baby took a great weight off Carrie's shoulders. They spent several hours discussing the ways in which the pregnancy would affect her career and how she would care for the baby afterwards. Adverse publicity made both of them shy away from admitting the truth for a while, and it was Bonnie's suggestion that Carrie take leave of absence from the ballet comapny, pleading physical exhaustion and mental collapse. She thought that only Gregory need know the truth, at least in the interim, and that Carrie's remaining months could be spent as quietly as possible, resting from the strain of dancing and preparing herself to face the public when it was all over.

Bonnie took care of everything. She told Gregory and wrote press releases sufficiently informative to keep the media happy, but vague enough so that the company couldn't be pinned down as to specifics. Carrie was safe from an unwanted telephone siege by the press because Bonnie had hired an answering service to handle the barrage. She did accept a spate of phone calls from various members of the company, expressing sympathy and concern, and a long one from Gregory whose attempt at hearty bluster didn't mask his disappointment. Carrie wept a little after hanging up, but then dried her eyes and set about sewing. To fill in her time, she had decided to make all her own maternity clothes. The thickening of her waistline was becoming more noticeable daily, and she was not sure how much longer she would fit in her ordinary clothes.

She forestalled anxious phone calls from her family by calling them herself before the news of her temporary retirement reached San Francisco via the gossip columns of the newspaper. She assured them that she was all right, but that her doctor had recommended a leave of absence after the rigours of her last tour. Elizabeth wanted to fly to New York, but Carrie told her that it wasn't necessary, that all she was doing was eating and sleeping and no one was to worry about her. It took a bit of persuading to convince her mother that there was no need for transatlantic plane journeys, and she had to promise to write frequently and phone if she wanted anything. Carrie finally got off the phone, wringing wet with sweat, her hands shaking and thinking that if she could get through an ordeal like that, she could survive anything.

Her days during the next week took on a steady, uncomplicated rhythm. She cooked all the meals, read novels and sewed during the day while Bonnie worked. She looked forward to Bonnie's arrival home to hear all the gossip, and she hung avidly on to every story about the successes or failures of the understudy who had replaced her. She even began to take an interest in the cocktail parties that Bonnie had to attend as part of her job. Like most dancers of her status, Carrie had often been invited to the parties that were part of the New York socialite scene, but had rarely gone, being too tired or too busy to find the time. Bonnie, on the other hand, found the parties useful. It was a way to meet potential backers for the company and massage the egos of those who had already donated time, effort or money to the cause.

Having napped during the afternoon, Carrie was usually awake when Bonnie came home from one of these affairs, and she would curl up on the divan and listen to the other girl talk about the party as she took off her make-up and got dressed for bed.

'I met the most fascinating man tonight,' Bonnie said one night, scrubbing off her eyeliner with a tissue.

Carrie smiled to herself. 'So what's new?'

'This one is different. He's all male.'

'That's what you said about David,' said Carrie, mentioning Bonnie's most recently discarded boy-friend.

Bonnie shrugged and threw the tissue in the waste-paper basket. 'David developed chinks in his virility, little cracks of weakness that grew into crevasses. He cried on my shoulder all the time.'

'Tell me about this one.'

'Tall, dark and gorgeous. A wonderful mouth—and you know how I go for sensual mouths!'

'What does he do?'

'Something vaguely aggressive for oil companies. I really didn't ask.'

Carrie, drowsy from her hot chocolate, stretched cat-like and then curled up again. 'What did you talk about?'

'Ballet; he was quite fascinated by my job, the company and you.'

Carrie yawned. 'Maybe he needs a tax deduction.'

Bonnie ran a brush through her hair. 'He isn't the type of man that a woman wants to spend the evening with talking about the Internal Revenue Service.'

'Are you going to spend an evening with him?'

'Friday night.'

Carrie shook her head in amazement. 'You're fast,' she teased.

Bonnie switched off the light over her make-up table and, turning around, gave Carrie an exaggerated, wicked wink. 'Just fast enough,' she said, 'to get caught.'

Bonnie's date arrived early on Friday evening while she was still getting dressed. Carrie had given instructions to the doorman of their building to send him up and she was waiting by the front door to answer it when the bell rang. She had been immersed in a novel all afternoon and was so deeply into the story that she opened the door with her mind only half on the man who stood before her, but at the sight of a pair of broad shoulders sheathed in a well-tailored silver-grey suit and dark eyes that held a brooding anger, her air of distraction completely disappeared.

'You!' she exclaimed, then tried to slam the door in Alex's face, but he was in the apartment and past her before she could do more than grab the doorknob.

'Not much of a welcome,' he commented drily.

'What are you doing here?' she hissed.

'Taking Bonnie to a Broadway show. She's not ready yet?' He glanced down the length of the hallway corridor.

Carrie glared at his handsome profile. 'This isn't fair to Bonnie.'

Alex looked back at her. 'What's not fair?'

'Taking her out when you're really interested in . . .' she faltered.

'Interested in you? You flatter yourself,' he said coldly. 'I liked Bonnie the minute I met her.'

Carrie had the feeling that she'd been knifed, a slicing blow with a sharp blade that took her breath away.

Alex took her sharp intake of breath as anger instead of humiliation. 'Our weekend *was* strictly casual, don't you agree?' he asked with a grim smile.

The knife took another twist. 'Yes,' she whispered.

'No contracts, no obligations,' he went on relentlessly. 'We merely shared a bed, some mutual pleasure and exploration.'

She winced inwardly, but she lifted her chin in an attempt at defence. 'We weren't in love with one another,' she said.

Alex leaned against the archway that led into the living room and stared at her, his eyes roving over the plait of her honey-brown hair and the loose white dress that successfully hid any sign of her growing waistline and made her look like a young girl. 'But we were lovers,' he said with sarcasm. 'I wonder why women want to make the distinction.'

'Because it's different,' she cried, stung by his mockery. 'Sex without love is meaningless.'

Alex's mouth slanted into a bitter line. 'So you've proved,' he grated.

'Alex darling, I hope I haven't kept you waiting for long, but I simply refuse to be on time. It's so pedestrian,' Bonnie said gaily, as she swept down the hall, elegant and sophisticated in a dove-grey silk dress with flowing sleeves and narrow skirt with a slit up one side. Her make-up was flawless and her hair gleamed under the overhead light like a metallic helmet. Carrie noticed that she was wearing her diamonds, a necklace with square-cut stones and a matching bracelet, earrings and ring.

'And you've met Carrie,' she continued, seemingly unaware of the tension in the air, although she gave Carrie a sharp look as if she wondered why Alex hadn't been invited to sit down and have a drink while he waited.

'Yes,' said Alex, 'I've had the pleasure.'

Bonnie pulled her fur coat out of the foyer closet, a dark ranch mink with a monogrammed silk lining, and handed it to Alex, who politely held it open for her. 'Alex was so curious about you,' she said to Carrie.

'Was he?' Carrie looked away from the derisive glint in Alex's eyes.

'I'm fascinated by ballet dancers,' he said smoothly. 'They have such dedication.'

Bonnie pulled her coat around her. 'Our ballerina is taking a well-deserved rest.'

Alex frowned. 'You're not dancing, Miss Moore?'

'I . . . I've been sick, and the doctor recommended that I take a few months off.'

'A small case of exhaustion,' Bonnie explained as she

picked up her bag from a small table. 'The Western tour was exceptionally rigorous.'

'What a shame,' said Alex, giving Carrie a cold smile. Your fans must miss you.'

'We all miss her,' Bonnie inserted loyally, 'but she'll be back soon.'

'Not soon enough for me,' Alex said silkily. 'I can't wait to see Miss Moore dance again.'

Carrie wondered why Alex had so much power to hurt her. Was it his intimate knowledge of her or the unborn baby that made her so vulnerable, causing her to tremble before the derision in his eyes? Everything he said was underlaid with a sarcasm and double meaning that made her cringe, but she couldn't afford to let him know how close he came to the wavering edge of her control.

'Have a good time,' she said, giving him a cool look from her amber eyes and turning away.

'Don't wait up,' said Bonnie, tugging at Carrie's plait of honey-brown hair as if she were a younger sister. 'We'll be late, won't we, darling?'

Alex's amused voice was deep and low. 'Do you want to paint the town red?'

'How did you guess?' Bonnie said with a laugh. 'Red is my favourite colour!'

They didn't come back until three in the morning. Carrie knew because she tossed and turned in her bed, searching desperately for an elusive sleep. Instead she found herself staring up at the dark ceiling, wondering what Bonnie and Alex were doing, imagining them laughing and dancing together, Alex's hand on the back of Bonnie's dress where it dipped in a daring plunge, Bonnie's head thrown back as she gave Alex one of her glittering looks. Bonnie knew, Carrie thought unhappily as she checked the lit numbers on her digital clock for the tenth time, how to make a man happy and wind him around her diamond-studded little finger.

It wasn't that she begrudged Bonnie her skill with

men. On the contrary, Carrie had long enjoyed watching her room-mate in action, but somehow it seemed different when the man was Alex. Carrie attributed her uneasiness about a relationship between Bonnie and Alex to his presence. She didn't want to answer the phone and hear his voice at the other end or open the door and see him standing there again. She couldn't bear many more conversations like the one they'd had earlier, and she certainly didn't want him around when her pregnancy became obvious. Carrie turned restlessly over on to one side and tugged the blankets up to her chin. All she wanted, she thought miserably, was to have Alex out of her life on a very permanent basis.

At quarter to three, she gave up her pursuit of a night's sleep and padded into the kitchen on her bare feet, clad in her long white nightgown, to make herself another cup of hot chocolate. The kitchen seemed cold and dreary under the fluorescent lights, and the insistent ticking of the stove clock was loud in the silence of the apartment. Carrie shivered a bit as she heated up the milk and, thankful when it finally came to a boil, poured in a spoonful of chocolate powder. She switched off the lights, held the steaming mug between both hands and was stepping into the hallway when the front door lock clicked. She froze in place, pressed against the wall, her heart beating in heavy, pounding thumps.

She could see the shadows of two people standing under the light in the foyer, the dark lengths angling down the hallway towards her so that they appeared to be upside down, their heads closest to her, the feet farthest away. The murmur of voices and low laughter drifted to her, and she strained to hear what they were saying, but the words were indistinct. Then the taller shadow bent its head and touched the shorter shadow on the mouth, and Carrie shut her eyes as tightly as she could. When she finally opened them again, the tall shadow was gone and she could hear Bonnie humming

to herself as she walked to her bedroom. Carrie scurried
to her own room, crept into bed and put down her hot
chocolate untouched. The sight of those shadows
touching had caused a pain to blossom in her chest like a
balloon that cut off her air supply, making her breath
come in rapid shallow gasps. It was a pain that didn't
diminish until the morning light came through her curtains, and she finally fell asleep from sheer and utter
exhaustion.

When the pain in her chest persisted as an ache, and her
shortness of breath caught her up at odd moments,
Carrie finally phoned the doctor. He called her in for an
examination, pronounced her healthy as a horse, if a bit
thin, and told her to avoid stress. Carrie went back to the
apartment and reflected that like all good advice, it was
easier said than done. How could she avoid stress when
Alex was calling and dating Bonnie? She was compelled
to be happy for Bonnie, who seemed to enjoy Alex's
company, and she was forced to listen to long rhapsodies
on his character. It seemed that, in addition to his good
looks, Alex was kind, considerate, intelligent, courteous
and polite. 'He sounds like a damned Boy Scout!' she
had finally snapped, and Bonnie had looked at her in
surprise and then gently suggested that she get some
rest.

Carrie tried to keep out of Alex's way when he came
to pick Bonnie up, but she wasn't always successful. One
evening, Bonnie was late coming home and Alex arrived
an hour early. Carrie, thinking it was a delivery man,
opened the door and found Alex standing there with a
child's party hat with red and green streamers in one
hand and a small bag of candies in the other.

'Celebrating your birthday?' she asked tartly, letting
him walk by her into the living room.

Alex lifted a dark eyebrow as if he found her humour
in bad taste and sat down on the couch, placing his fawn

coat beside him. The living room was a cosy place, decorated in gold and brown velvet with a four-seater couch in a wide semi-circle before a fireplace. Carrie sat down opposite him, being too polite to leave before Bonnie returned, but hating every moment that she had to be in his presence. She clenched her hands together and sat in a rigid pose, dressed in a yellow overblouse and blue cords, her last pair of slacks to fit. Her hair, loosely brushed away from her face, fell down her back in a curtain of golden-brown waves.

'My nephew has just turned six,' Alex said as he put the hat and bag down on the coffee table between them. The bag tilted sideways, pouring a handful of jelly beans and chocolate kisses on to the table's glass surface.

'I didn't know you had one,' Carrie responded, her indifference only marginally shaded by a polite interest.

Alex sat back, stretching his long legs before him. He was wearing a dark blue suit, white shirt and muted tie. The lamp beside him cast a light on to his hair, causing it to gleam an obsidian black. 'My twin brother's son.'

Unintentionally, Carrie sat up straighter. 'You have a twin?'

Alex gave her a mocking look. 'Don't sound so horrified. Is two of us more than you can bear?'

Carrie didn't know how to express her feeling that Alex came out of nowhere like a vengeful god, without the ordinary human ties of friend and family. 'I didn't know that you had a brother here in Manhattan,' she said weakly.

'He's a doctor, married to a wonderful woman and has three nice kids.'

Was there a tinge of envy in Alex's voice? Carrie couldn't tell and she unconsciously wrung her hands. 'He sounds very settled.'

'As opposed to me, you mean.' The dark eyes were amused.

'Well, you aren't really.'

'Never found the right woman.'

Carrie avoided the obvious insinuation. 'Most women don't want to travel to the places that your job takes you.'

Alex shrugged. 'I don't have to travel. I do it by choice now.'

An awkward silence stretched out between them while Carrie desperately sought another topic of conversation. Finally she cleared her throat and said, 'And your parents?'

'My father's retired. He and my mother live in North Carolina near the barrier islands. He loves to fish.'

'That's interesting.'

His mouth slanted. 'Is it?'

She gave him a cold, amber glance. 'I am trying to be polite,' she said through clenched teeth.

Alex leaned back and crossed his arms over his broad chest. 'Why try so hard? Why not admit that you hate my guts?'

'I don't hate your guts. I would simply prefer,' Carrie said carefully, 'not to see you.'

'You know,' he said in a musing voice, 'you could learn a few lessons from Bonnie. We met one of her previous lovers at a restaurant and she handled it very well. You would have thought they were best friends.'

'Bonnie has a bit more experience than I do.'

'Really? I thought you were trying to catch up.'

'What does that mean?' Carrie asked angrily.

'Your boy-friend Casimir. Or has he dropped you since you left? I hear from Bonnie that he's very fickle.'

Carrie lifted her chin. 'We're friends now.' It seemed the safest response. She didn't want to nurture one lie with another and preferred to let Alex think that she and Casimir had parted company.

'That didn't last long.'

'It was by mutual choice,' she said defensively.

Alex leaned forward, suddenly dangerous in his intent, the skin hard and taut over his cheekbones. 'Tell me, do you just get a charge out of casual sex?'

The dull ache in her chest amplified into a sharp pain, and she stood up abruptly. 'If you don't mind, I have a phone call to make,' she said breathlessly.

Alex gave her a long, ironic look. 'Don't let me stop you,' he said. 'I don't mind waiting for Bonnie by myself.'

It was now quite obvious to Carrie that she had to leave New York. She didn't want to tell Bonnie that Alex was the father of her baby, and she could see no way of convincing her that she shouldn't be dating him. Bonnie had already sensed Carrie's antipathy towards Alex, had commented on it and then wisely avoided the topic after Carrie had assured her, effusively and at great length, that she *did* like Alex, that she thought he was a wonderful man, *very* suitable for Bonnie, that they made a great couple and how could Bonnie *ever* think such a thing.

'You seem so uncomfortable when he's around,' Bonnie had explained.

'I don't want to interfere,' Carrie protested. 'I hate to be a third wheel.'

'You're not a third wheel yet,' Bonnie said wryly. 'So far nothing's happened between the sheets.'

'Really?' Carrie croaked.

'I wonder if I'm losing my touch,' Bonnie said musingly, then shrugged. 'Who knows? Maybe, for all those virile good looks, Alex Taylor is undersexed.'

Carrie had fled to her bedroom and buried her head under the pillow. She didn't know whether she was laughing in hysteria, relief or just the total irony of it all, but it was one of the few lighthearted moments that she had had in a week of despair. She had gone through one plan after another for leaving Manhattan and discarded them all. She couldn't explain to Bonnie why she was leaving; she didn't want to go to her parents in San Francisco; and she had no idea where she could stay. Just when she had got to the point of feeling frantic, help arrived from a surprising and unexpected corner.

Veronica, who had been out of town for a month, visited Carrie as soon as she returned and learned the truth from Gregory. Her arrival brought a wave of nostalgia. The sight of those strong features, implacable dark eyes and the slender dancer's body in its usual black leotard and denim skirt made Carrie throw her arms around Veronica, even though she knew how much the older ballerina hated displays of sentimentality.

Veronica tolerated the hug and then held Carrie off at arm's length. 'You look terrible,' she said critically, eyeing Carrie's too slender face and the dark circles under her eyes. 'All bones. Are you eating?'

'I don't have morning sickness any more,' Carrie said evasively. Although the nausea had gone, her appetite had never really come back. She couldn't do more than pick at her food; nothing seemed appealing. The doctor had given her a pregnancy diet to follow, and Carrie was faithful about getting down the basic requirements, but beyond that she didn't eat a thing.

Veronica pursed her lips and shook her head. 'And it doesn't look like you're getting any sleep either. If you want to have a healthy baby and dance again, you're going to have to do something about yourself.'

Carrie led her into the living room where they sat down on the couch. 'Between you and Bonnie, I'm being mothered to death,' she said with a smile.

Veronica took out a pin from her greying chignon and tucked it back in impatiently. 'You are coming back to the company, aren't you?' she asked.

To Carrie the future was hazy, a dense, impenetrable fog with no coherence or guidelines. 'I don't know,' she confessed.

'Other dancers have had babies and returned.'

'I know that, but I'm not . . .' She paused, unable to articulate her emotions.

'You're mixed up, confused and could use a breath of fresh air.'

Carrie gave Veronica a thankful look. 'The apartment does seem claustrophic sometimes.'

'Why don't you spend some time at my beach house in the Rockaways? It's comfortable, right on the ocean and the sea breeze might put some colour into your cheeks.'

'Are you sure?' Carrie asked hesitantly. 'I thought you closed it up for the winter.'

'Not this year. I stay on the weekends.' Veronica leaned forward and took Carrie's hands gently between hers. 'Why not go? I'd enjoy your company. Say yes.'

Veronica would never know how welcome her invitation was or how desperate Carrie had been. She could hardly believe that the solution to her problem was so close at hand; she had the relieved feeling of a drowning victim who has been offered an unforeseen lifeline. 'Yes,' she said, 'I'd love to.'

CHAPTER FIVE

CARRIE felt the baby move during her first week at Veronica's beach house. That slight flutter, almost too faint to make an impression, happened while she was walking along the edge of the beach, watching the constant roll of dark green waves pounding against the white sand. She stopped dead in her tracks and waited for it to return and, in a few minutes, she felt it again, life stirring and moving within her. She imagined the baby kicking or punching with its tiny fists, and there was a tightening in her throat and chest as if the joy of it could strangle her.

The wind off the water picked up the strands of her hair and threw them across her mouth as she stood there, and the breeze was strong enough to flatten her windbreaker against her swelling abdomen. She had been walking barefoot with her jeans rolled up, digging her toes into the cool sand and enjoying the emptiness of the beach and the wild cries of black and white gulls, wheeling overhead, following her in the hope of food. Now she sat down, curled her hands into the sand and, lifting them, watched the fine grains trickle through her fingers.

She was, she realised suddenly as she watched the waves crash against the beach and send dark arcs of water up the sand, happy for the first time in months. The pain in her chest had disappeared, and it came to her that she had been stifling in Bonnie's apartment, pressured by Alex's presence and uncertain about her life. For some reason, the ocean and the beach made her feel stronger about her decisions and more convinced that she had been right to see the pregnancy through and not tell Alex that he was the father. The air, the water and the sky were so elemental; there was a feeling of eternity in this particular corner of the universe, and Carrie felt as if she were part of an endless cycle with the steady drumming of the waves in her ears and the salty taste of her skin from the mist-coated breeze.

Her problems seemed minuscule in the vastness before her. There were babies born every second, and the news of hers would cause no more than a small ripple in the scheme of things. She would survive it all; the insatiable curiosity of the press, her family's disappointment, even the difficulties of being a single parent. The determination and perseverance that had made her a prima ballerina wouldn't desert her, and she threw back her head and laughed at a gull that swept down to land before her, exulting in a sudden feeling of wellbeing and happiness. 'Baby,' she whispered to that unknown being, stretching and moving within her, 'we're going to be just fine!'

The good feeling lasted all through the next week as Carrie made herself more and more at home in Veronica's house. It was a small, two-bedroom place with faded wooden shingles and old, but comfortable furniture that stood on a narrow side street five minutes from the beach. The kitchen and bathroom hadn't been modernised, but they weren't so primitive as to be uncomfortable. What Carrie liked best about the house, next to its proximity to the ocean, was the enclosed front porch. She would wrap herself up in a jacket and blanket and spend the afternoon on the chaise-longue, reading but most often sleeping. She would awaken feeling refreshed by the cool ocean air and, with more enthusiasm than she had felt for months, would make herself dinner.

The locals were a tight-knit group but friendly, particularly Mrs Jones who ran the small grocery at the corner and Mr Finch, her next-door neighbour. When the portly Mrs Jones found out that Carrie was a ballet dancer just like Miss Timberlake, she insisted on giving her a small discount. Carrie tried to explain that she wasn't starving, but Mrs Jones had read somewhere that dancers are underpaid and overworked. 'You just have to eat proper,' she said, and Carrie reluctantly agreed, although she decided to save some of her free ballet tickets for Mrs Jones, having a suspicion that a similar arrangement had been established with Veronica.

Mr Finch was a tall, thin elderly man with a shock of white hair that never stayed down, fierce blue eyes under bushy eyebrows and a scrawny neck with a large Adam's apple. He was a widower and fond of sitting out on his front porch watching the world go by. He had taken good notice of Carrie's arrival, and she was positive that he had her schedule down pat by her second day there. He was certainly right on the spot when the screened porch door fell off its hinges after being blown open by the wind. Carrie came out when she heard the noise of it falling to the ground and was vainly trying to hold the door up and push the pin into the hinge at the same time when Mr Finch arrived with a hammer.

'No problem,' he muttered. 'No problem.'

Carrie stepped aside as he efficiently hammered the pin back in and then tested the door a couple of times to make sure it worked. 'That's very kind of you,' she said.

'Ain't right for a lady in your condition to be repairing.'

She glanced at him in surprise and looked down at her stomach. She was wearing a thin blouse over maternity jeans and its folds enclosed a small but definite mound. Usually she wore heavy sweaters or her windbreaker which hid the growing evidence of her pregnancy.

'The wife and I, we had six. All boys,' Mr Finch explained gruffly.

'Oh, how nice.'

Mr Finch ran a gnarled hand through his white hair. 'Now that depends on how they all turned out. I got four good ones and two that are middling.'

'Middling?'

'Not working. Living off the government like them sultans of Turkey.'

Carrie restrained a smile. 'Really?' she asked.

Over a shared coffee, Mr Finch proved to be garrulous, opinionated and warmhearted. He regaled Carrie with long stories about his boyhood in Texas, his marriage, his children and all the ways he had helped Miss Timberlake with repairs on the beach house. They were friends after that, waving hello and visiting occasionally. Carrie soon came to appreciate what a good handyman Mr Finch was. He fixed the stove when it went on the blink and replaced a broken window pane in the kitchen. He refused to accept money, but Carrie repaid him with food, baking cookies and cakes which he devoured with relish. He showed only a modest curiosity about Carrie's life, accepting without question the story she fabricated about her husband who worked in the city and was too swamped with work to visit.

Veronica kept true to her plans and came down on the weekends to see how Carrie was doing, noticing immediately the difference that the ocean air had made in her appearance, appetite and wellbeing.

'The house agrees with you,' she said with a pleased look.

Carrie smiled at her. They were making dinner in comfortable companionship after having spent the afternoon taking a long walk down the beach. 'I really needed to get away from New York.'

Veronica gave her a long look over a tomato she was slicing. 'Is the father there?'

'No . . . yes,' Carrie stammered, unwilling to lie to Veronica who had been so kind and had never once reproached her or asked embarrassing questions. 'He hasn't any idea about the baby. I don't see him.'

'Then it isn't Casimir.'

'Of course not!'

'Thank heavens for that. He's been talking about you constantly. I think he's obsessed.'

'I never would sleep with him; it drove him crazy.'

'In his case, it's a short trip,' said Veronica, her mouth twisted into an expression of distaste.

'He's really not all that bad,' Carrie urged.

'Pah!' Veronica spat the word out. 'He's an actor, not a dancer!'

They fell into a conversation about ballet, but later that night, long after Veronica had returned to New York, Carrie suddenly realised that she hadn't thought about the company in days. She had, at first, missed the dancing with an almost physical pang, but now she often forgot for long periods of time that she had ever been a dancer at all. The ballet world seemed to be far in the distance, a bit hazy and out of focus. The intrigues and gossip, the affairs and the plans, all seemed quite foreign to her as if they were part of another country, another reality.

She grew daily more and more involved with the changes in her body. The movement of the baby, the heaviness in her breasts, the darkening of her nipples and her slowly increasing girth seemed to be more fascinating than anything else. She read the news with indifference and never turned the radio on. Time had slowed down for her, a lazy circle of sleeping and waking, walking and resting, and all the time, having a feeling of such amazing power that she was carrying this infant, nourishing it, cradling it in her body.

So uninterested was she in the outside world that even the arrival of a telegram failed to stir her. It came to the grocery store, which also served as the local post office, and Mrs Jones bustled over to deliver it.

'A telegram!' she cried outside the door.

Carrie opened it and smiled. 'Come on in.'

But Mrs Jones, plump, grey-haired and aproned

under her coat, stood on the porch and stared. 'Lordy, but you're pregnant!' she exclaimed in astonishment.

It no longer alarmed Carrie to have anyone notice the obvious. In fact, she had got to the point where she would have been offended if her state passed without notice. It was so important to her that she felt as if she must have the word PREGNANT blazoned on her forehead. 'Yes,' she said. 'Would you like some coffee?'

Mrs Jones, of course, wouldn't have missed a chance of grilling Carrie for anything. She sat down at the table, having put the now forgotten telegram in an apron pocket, and proceeded to bombard her with questions. Carrie, thankful for the gold band she had purchased in New York before leaving, told her the same story she had told Mr Finch, which somewhat more embroidery and flowery detail.

'Well,' said Mrs Jones, pursing her lips and putting her coffee down on the table, 'I do think your husband should get down here a bit more often and keep an eye on you. I've had three myself.'

'Veronica comes down, and I have Mr Finch.'

Mrs Jones waved off the suggestion of Mr Finch with a brisk motion of her hand. 'Howard's a dear, but the man wouldn't know the first thing about a miscarriage.'

Carrie gave a dreamy smile. 'I'm as healthy as a horse.'

'You never can tell and . . . good heavens, I forgot to give you the telegram!'

Carrie took it from her and, opening it, read it slowly and then once again much more quickly, her face turning pale.

'Bad news?' Mrs Jones asked avidly.

'I . . .' Carrie took a deep breath, then gave Mrs Jones a brilliant, well-staged smile. 'My sister's coming for a visit.'

'Now, isn't that nice?' said Mrs Jones, beaming. 'She'll keep you company.'

Elizabeth Moore, it seemed, had literally worried herself sick over Carrie and come down with pneumonia. She had insisted that Julie fly to New York and find out what really was happening, and the family, eager to keep her calm and happy, had agreed. Julie had phoned the apartment and got hold of Bonnie, who had tried desperately, Carrie later learned, to lead her off the track. But Julie, who had just as much push and shove as Bonnie, smelled something fishy and finally weaseled Carrie's address out of her.

She flew immediately out from San Francisco, rented a car in New York and drove to the Rockaways, arriving a day after the telegram. Carrie, who had suffered from an extremely bad night, felt more nervous and apprehensive than she ever had before a major performance. If Julie were only visiting for an afternoon, she could hide her pregnancy under heavy clothes, but her sister was going to stay for five days, the telegram had announced, and Carrie knew there was no way of concealing her condition. So she decided to be up-front and honest about it and was standing just inside the front door, wearing maternity slacks and a checked maternity blouse, when Julie drove up. She fought a feeling of panic as her sister got out from the car, but forced herself to smile as she opened the door.

'Julie,' she smiled, 'it's good to see you.'

Julie stepped into the porch with a wide smile. 'Carrie! You look great, I don't know why . . .' The words trailed away as her eyes travelled from Carrie's face to her waistline. 'My God!' she whispered.

'Obvious, isn't it?' Carrie said ruefully.

Julie shook her head in stunned disbelief.

'I'm happy about it,' Carrie said defensively. 'Very happy.'

'But who . . . ?'

'It doesn't matter.'

The two sisters looked at one another, one nervously

defiant, the other incredulous, then Julie began to laugh and threw her arms around Carrie. 'Join the club,' she said with a gasp, 'I'm pregnant, too!'

Dealing with Julie was both easier and more difficult than Carrie had anticipated. They talked a lot about pregnancy, comparing symptoms and experiences, and Carrie realised how much she missed having a close woman friend who could be supportive and understanding. But they also argued, particularly over two issues, the first being their parents. Julie insisted that neither Elizabeth or Joshua would be as shocked or as upset as Carrie thought.

'They weren't born in the Dark Ages,' she said one afternoon as they strolled along the beach, watching the way the sun glinted in the water, turning it the colour of old jade. 'They know about things like sex and babies.'

'But I don't plan to get married.'

'Carrie, they love you. Sure, they're going to be upset to a degree, but they're not going to disown you. Besides, Mom adores babies. She's already ecstatic about Ryan, thrilled that I'm pregnant again, and I'm sure, once she gets over the initial shock, she'll be excited about your baby. You have no idea how she brags about her family to her friends! Half of them have grown-up children who either don't believe in marriage or plan to remain childless. Mom's going to feel like her cup's running over, with three grandchildren.'

'But won't they be hurt that I just slept with someone and didn't plan to . . .'

Julie gave her a wicked grin. 'I lived with David for four months before we even decided to get married.'

'You did! Why didn't they tell me?'

'Mom didn't want you to get any ideas.'

'See, she didn't like it.'

'But the point is, Carrie, that it didn't kill her, and Dad once told me that he thought it might not be a bad idea for couples to live together first and see if the relationship could stand the strain. I know he was trying hard to be modern, but at least he *was* trying.'

'Oh, Julie, I don't know,' Carrie said doubtfully.

The second topic of dissension was the baby's father. It hadn't taken Julie more than a minute to figure out that Alex Taylor was the man responsible, and she thought Carrie was being extremely foolish not to tell him.

'He's the kind of man who would want to know,' she pointed out.

Carrie looked at her in astonishment. 'How would you know that?' she asked.

They were lying side by side on the porch on a pair of chaise-longues that they had pulled to one side to be in the path of the morning sun. Julie turned over so that she face Carrie, pulling her own honey-brown hair back over one ear. 'Because I've met him several times.'

'You have!' exclaimed Carrie.

'He visits Mom and Dad when he's in San Francisco.'

Carrie was literally struck dumb and gaped at her sister.

'He's not at all indifferent to you, no matter what you think,' Julie said with a smile at her sister's obvious stupefaction.

'But I told you that he's going out with Bonnie!'

Julie shrugged. 'It doesn't mean anything, they could be just friends.'

'Highly unlikely,' Carrie said.

'Well, is the relationship deeper? Are they sleeping together?'

Carrie opened her mouth, then shut it again, re-membering Bonnie's disgust over Alex's apparent lack of interest in sex. She had automatically assumed that he and Bonnie would be having an affair; her room-mate never shrank from sex, rather she seemed to revel in it, but Julie had put a seed of doubt in Carrie's mind and a little flare of hope leapt in her chest. 'I don't think they are,' she said in a musing voice.

'There!' Julie said triumphantly. 'Perhaps he's merely going out with her so he can keep tabs on you.'

It seemed to make sense until Carrie remembered, with depressing clarity, the derision in Alex's eyes the last time they had spoken and the cold tone of his voice. 'I don't want Alex to know,' she said dully, watching the bare branches of a tree that stood outside the porch enclosure bend and creak in the wind. 'And promise me you won't say anything.'

Julie made a motion over her chest. 'Cross my heart.'

Carrie turned quickly to her sister. 'I mean it!' she said vehemently.

'Carrie,' Julie said softly, 'I would never interfere.'

Carrie was immediately contrite. 'I'm sorry,' she said. 'I know you wouldn't.'

'And I won't say anything to Mom and Dad either. I'll just tell them that you look great and you're getting a lot of rest. You'll have to tell them about the baby when you're good and ready.'

Carrie took one of Julie's hands in hers. 'Have I told you what a good sister you are?' she said thankfully.

'Nope,' said Julie with a grin. 'Not since I saved you from Bobby Roper's baseball bat!'

After Julie had gone, Carrie took a train into Manhattan and visited her doctor for a check-up. He was delighted with her progress and the baby's development. Carrie celebrated the good news by purchasing a large man's Arctic sweater and a voluminous slicker. She didn't want to give up her walks on the beach because of the increasingly foul weather. She found that she liked to watch the ocean even when it was angry, the waves high and turbulent, their tops capped in foam.

She met Bonnie for lunch in a pleasant restaurant with oaken beams and hanging green plants. They shared news over soup and a salad and talked about the company. Carrie was surprised to learn that Casimir had taken to hanging around the apartment, presumably waiting for her return, but in reality eating Bonnie out of house and home.

'A man of gargantuan appetites,' Bonnie said drily as she picked a mushroom out of her salad.

'He must be between girl-friends.'

'The company is buzzing with the gossip. It would seem that our Casanova is languishing. Not even our new little corps members seem to interest him.'

'Maybe his tastes have changed to older women,' Carrie suggested with a smile.

Bonnie shuddered delicately. 'If you mean me, Carrie, then please get your mind out of the gutter. I wouldn't touch that oaf with a ten-foot pole! He has about as much finesse as a bull in a china closet. Anyway, he claims that you've broken his heart.'

'He knows about the baby!'

Bonnie shook her head. 'No one knows except Gregory, Veronica and myself. Believe me, your secret is safe.'

Carrie took another spoonful of soup. 'And Alex?' she asked casually. 'Are you still dating him?'

She looked up to catch a moody look on Bonnie's face. 'He's been out of town for weeks.'

Carrie knew how much Bonnie hated to be left high and dry. 'Are you going out with anyone else?' she asked.

'No, I've been keeping Casimir company watching television,' Bonnie said with disgust, then gave a small, smug smile. 'But Alex is due back today and I hope to see him tonight.'

There was an unmistakable glitter in her blue eyes, one that Carrie had seen before. It meant that Bonnie was ready for the kill, and Carrie suddenly had a wave of pain break in her chest. 'I see,' she said, looking down as if she were concentrating on her soup and trying to blink back the tears. She had thought that pain like that could only come from a physical source, never realising before that jealousy had its own sharp, pointed blade.

She returned to the beach house on the train, feeling wretched and miserable. She didn't want to be jealous of Bonnie, her closest friend and her room-mate. Bonnie didn't know about her affair with Alex or that he was the father of her baby. If she did, Carrie knew that she would back away and announce a hands-off policy. If there was one thing Bonnie believed in, it was steering clear of another woman's man. She didn't mind the confused tangle of dating more than one man at a time, but she was scrupulous about not getting involved in messy triangles.

But knowing that Bonnie's heart was in the right place didn't make Carrie feel any better. She couldn't sleep that night for thinking about Alex visiting Bonnie in the apartment. The memories of their own lovemaking came back in full and excruciating force, and she cringed when she thought of him touching the other woman. And Bonnie was so experienced. Alex was probably finding sex with her far more satisfying than it had ever been with Carrie, who hadn't known anything but her own inadequate instincts.

Carrie sat up in bed and listened to the distant, soothing sound of the ocean, but even that didn't make her feel better. She'd never really been this jealous of anyone before—not in her career where she had risen like a meteoric star or among her family where she felt loved and cherished. It was a new and awful feeling, destructive and hurtful. It pressed on her chest and twisted its knife in her heart. It made her breath come in gasps, and she knew that it wasn't good for either her or the baby, who had become suddenly very active, those formerly tiny flutters now distinct taps.

Carrie lay down again to sleep, determined to keep

her mind on subjects more pleasant. She mapped out the next day's activities, planned a grocery list and decided to bake in the morning. Mr Finch would like a pineapple upside-down cake and so would she. She had developed a bit of a sweet tooth now that she was no longer dancing and being frantic about her weight. A pineapple upside-down cake and chocolate chip cookies, maybe banana bread or apple sauce cake. Carrie finally fell asleep to a vision of strawberry shortcake. Her last drowsy thought was that strawberries were out of season, but she was, by then, far too tired to care.

Her grandiose baking plans were reduced to a sensible level by the light of day, the restrictions of the kitchen and her limited provisions. In the morning, she made a carrot cake and indulged in a large helping with lunch. After a short nap, she got dressed and put on her new sweater and raincoat. The weather had turned decidedly nasty; dark clouds rolled on the horizon and a cold wind bent the slender tree in the front yard over like a bow. Carrie braided her hair into two long plaits and tucked them into the hood of her coat. She covered the carrot cake with foil and then heard the sound of rain beating against the window. 'Damn,' she muttered to herself, and added another layer of plastic wrap. Mr Finch wasn't going to enjoy soggy cake.

He was, as she had guessed he would be, pleased as Punch, and set the package down on the kitchen table. His house was smaller than Veronica's and neat as a pin.

'Some coffee?' he offered in return.

'No, thanks.' Carrie had once sampled Mr Finch's coffee and knew better than to try it a second time. He believed in a strong, thick brew, the kind that could hold a spoon perpendicular and was reputed to put hair on a man's chest. 'I'm going for a walk.'

'It ain't too nice out there.'

Carrie glanced out a window. 'No, but the rain has stopped and . . .'

Mr Finch glanced at her face and stood up to look out the window as well. 'You've got a visitor,' he said. 'And he sure travels in style.'

The car was a low-slung silver-grey and the man who was getting out had black hair and very broad shoulders. 'Yes, he does,' Carrie said faintly.

'It's nice that your hubby got a chance to visit.'

Carrie turned to him with the words of denial on her lips, but failed to say them. What difference did it make who Mr Finch thought Alex was? 'I guess I'd better get going,' she said.

'Now, are you sure he wouldn't like some of this here carrot cake?' Mr Finch asked with a wrinkled frown as he followed her to the door.

Carrie shook her head. 'Enjoy it, Mr Finch. I made it for you.'

As she walked towards Alex, the wind tugging out tendrils of hair from her braids, Carrie got angrier and angrier. She cursed Bonnie for telling him where she was and she cursed Alex for having the nerve to come when he knew she didn't want to see him. By the time she had reached her porch door where Alex was waiting for her, she had built herself up into a righteous fury. 'What are you doing here?' she demanded.

Alex shook his head in mock admiration. 'You really have a way of making a man feel welcome!' He paused. 'Do I get invited in?'

She gave an indifferent shrug. 'You can go in if you want, but I'm going for a walk on the beach.' Going in meant taking off the oversized man's sweater and her tent-like slicker. Underneath she was wearing a pair of maternity jeans and an old, stretched-out turtleneck that quite snugly enveloped her stomach. Without her outer clothes, she knew that she looked distinctly pregnant.

Alex raised a dark eyebrow but merely said, 'I'll go with you. Hold on while I zip up my jacket.'

He was dressed in blue jeans, fawn desert boots and a beige jacket with a nylon exterior. The wind which buffeted her back and forth didn't seem to affect him at all, except for his hair, which blew in an attractive fashion across his forehead. It occurred to Carrie, in a moment of irony, that if she'd deliberately hand-picked a candidate to be the father of her child, she couldn't have chosen better than Alex. If passed on, those dark eyes, the incisive cut of his mouth and the square angle of his jaw would make a beautiful child. She deliberately pushed the thought aside and began walking, bending her head against the wind and watching her boots take one step after another on the pavement. She didn't check if Alex was following her, but she didn't need to. His proximity alone made the hairs rise on the back of her neck.

'Do you walk often?' he asked, coming up alongside her, his hands tucked into his pockets.

'Every day,' she said curtly.

'It must suit you. You look very healthy.'

Carrie ignored the compliment.

'You'll be dancing soon, won't you?'

She lifted her shoulders, then dropped them again in a negative fashion. 'I don't know.'

'You mean you're no longer interested in your career?' Alex asked persistently.

'I just burnt out for a while.'

'I thought it was your whole life,' he persisted.

'I needed to get away,' Carrie said curtly.

They arrived at the beach and she turned away from him to walk by the water's edge. She was so disturbed at his presence that she couldn't even begin to be polite. So she followed the breakers, greyish-black under the dark sky, thankful that their roar made conversation almost impossible. But Alex tucked his hand under her elbow and leaned close enough to speak into her ear. 'This reminds me of my boyhood,' he remarked.

Carrie gave him a quick glance. 'Does it?'

'I grew up in the Hamptons.'

She knew the area; it was on the south coast of eastern Long Island, and the rich lived there in large, beautiful homes with the wide beach and ocean as their front lawns.

'My brother and I spent every minute we could in the water. We even tried to go skinny-dipping during the winter. I got pneumonia and my brother, Andrew, got punished.' Alex grinned at the memory, and Carrie had a sudden vision of two black-haired, tanned-skinned boys playing in the ocean, jumping through the breakers.

'Your parents must have loved that,' she commented.

'They were used to shenanigans. Andrew and I were always in trouble and always having accidents. I thought everyone broke a bone on a yearly basis when they grew up.'

Carrie looked at him in horror and thought of the baby, now busily pounding its fist against her stomach. Was her child going to be a hell-raiser like Alex? 'You broke a bone every year?'

'Sometimes more than one. Every doctor and nurse in the emergency room knew us. They called us "the terrible two."'

'Maybe you were accident-prone?'

Alex laughed into the wind, showing his strong white teeth. 'No,' he said, 'I never had another accident after I discovered girls.'

'And when was that?' she asked acerbically. 'When you were twelve?'

Alex glanced at her. 'You don't have a very good opinion of me.'

'Should I?'

'What would you say if I told you that I've never made

a promise to a woman that I didn't keep and that every one of my lovers has parted with me on good terms?'

Carrie felt herself stiffen at the mention of his lovers. How many had he had? Five, ten, twenty, a hundred? 'Aren't you lucky that you have so many good friends?' she asked mockingly, refraining from the obvious fact that she was the exception to his rule.

'Not so many,' he said soberly. 'I'm a one-woman man and I don't care for one-night stands.'

'But marriage isn't on your agenda either.'

Alex gave her a quizzical look, but his tone was serious. 'Let's put it this way. I take marriage very seriously. It's an institution that requires commitment, love and caring on the part of two very compatible people. When I decide to marry, it will be for ever.'

Carrie wondered why he was telling her all this. 'Are you trying to tell me that Naples was an exception to your rule?' she asked angrily.

Alex gave a thoughtful pause. 'I don't like what happened in Naples,' he said slowly. 'It didn't turn out the way I wanted.'

Carrie bit her lip and looked out across the thrashing ocean to the almost indistinct horizon where the dark water met the dark sky. Their affair in Florida hadn't turned out to the satisfaction of anyone. Alex had been unable to pursue their affair into something more meaningful than a weekend fling, and her life now resembled the ocean before her; turbulent, erratic and stormy. She felt the baby stir within her, the tangible and poignant link between herself and the tall man beside her.

'I'm sorry,' she said, her tone more wistful than she intended.

'Carrie?' Alex stopped her, his hand on her arm, and turned her slowly so that they faced one another, the ocean at her back, loose tendrils of hair whipping across her face.

'You'd better go back to New York,' she said.

'I wanted to talk to you, to get past the bitterness. I thought . . .'

She looked away from the intensity in his dark eyes. 'I don't want to talk to you.'

His hands gripped her shoulders, painfully. 'I know from Bonnie that you're not a woman who takes things lightly. Yet you acted as if that weekend in Florida meant nothing!'

Carrie forced herself to look up. 'Because it didn't mean anything. I had a career to worry about. I didn't need a lover.'

A muscle clenched in the hard line of his jaw. 'But you're not dancing now, and you don't even know if you'll be going back.'

She shrugged. 'Time will tell.'

'Carrie.'

The word was soft, as was the touch of his finger along her mouth, tracing the outline of her lips. It held her there, immobilised, not speaking, her breath quickening. He bent his head over hers, kissing where his finger had been, his lips gentle on hers. Carrie's hands came up and rested on his shoulders, feeling their strength beneath the fabric of his jacket. She had forgotten how her body responded to Alex's touch; her memories, she found, were only pale evocations of reality.

His mouth tasted of ocean salt, his lips were warm and sweet against hers. When he pulled her closer to him, she moved easily into the circle of his arms, stretching upwards on her toes to run her fingers through the tangled, damp strands of his hair. Her eyes closed as other sensations took over. The ocean roared in her ears, the wind tugged the hood off her head, but all she felt was the movement of his mouth on hers, the sensuous caress of his palms down her back, the arch of her body meeting his hard length.

His mouth left hers to light on an eyelid, the soft skin

at her temple, the shell-like curve of her ear. 'I've wanted this,' he murmured, his breath warming her cheek. 'I thought we'd never . . .'

His breath caught in his throat and his hands stopped in their slow climb up her sides to her breasts. Carrie, lost in sensation, blinked at the sudden stiffness of his body and his swift rejection as he pushed her away.

'You're pregnant.' The voice was flat; the eyes were burning her.

Carrie could barely swallow. 'Yes.'

'Why the hell didn't you tell me?' he asked harshly.

The lie came easily to her. Perhaps she had planned it during the night when she had had the nightmare. It had been a feverish dream of exposure and fear, of Alex being able to see within her to the baby, of his hand breaking through her skin to take it from her. She had woken from it to find the sheets damp with sweat, her heart pounding as if she had been running for her life. As it was now, when she could hear the drumming of her pulse louder than the waves crashing down behind her.

'The baby isn't yours,' she said coldly.

Alex was silent for a minute, his eyes searching her face, looking deeply into hers, their amber shaded by dark eyelashes coated with mist. 'Are you telling me the truth?' he grated.

'It's Casimir Rudenko's baby. That's why I left the ballet. I didn't want him to know.'

Suddenly, Alex raised both hands up and tightened them into brutal fists as if he would hit her in his anger. Carrie cringed and backed away, frightened by the loathing and fury in his eyes. He saw the motion and gave a harsh laugh. 'I don't hit women,' he said, through clenched teeth. 'I've been brought up to be a damned gentleman.'

'I'm sorry—' she began.

'The hell you are,' he grated, his face bleaker than the grey sky over his head. 'The hell you are!'

He turned then and walked away, the heel of his boot leaving a deep indentation in the wet sand. Carrie watched the harsh angle of his shoulders until she could no longer see him, and then she drooped, her hands hanging loosely at her side, her head bent, braids falling beside her pale cheeks. The lie had come so easily to her that she wondered why the truth had taken so long to reveal itself. She loved Alex; she had fallen in love with him the moment he had walked towards her on that patio at the hotel, his hair gleaming like obsidian under the Florida moon. It was an emotion that explained everything; her jealousy and the attraction that she fought whenever he was near. Love had been there all along, rooted in her heart, growing secretly beneath the surface of her life and waiting to spring into full bloom under the passionate touch of his lips.

CHAPTER SIX

Carrie went into premature labour during the middle of that night. She awoke, feeling a painful twinge on one side that grew into full-scale wrenching contractions within a few hours. At first, she desperately tried to will the pains away as if they were a figment of her imagination, but they persisted, causing her breath to come in shallow gasps and her hands to tighten until her nails broke through the skin of her palms. She fought them with every ounce of will power she possessed, only to discover that rigid resistance made the pain more powerful. Finally, she was reduced to twisting on the bed, trying to find a position that would ease the ever stronger contractions, terrified of what they meant. She had just begun her sixth month of pregnancy, and she didn't need any sophisticated medical expertise to know that a baby born that prematurely faced little chance of survival.

With despair, she admitted defeat at dawn and crawled out of bed, pulled on some clothes and made her way slowly two blocks to the grocery store, wishing for the first time that Veronica had had a telephone installed in the beach house. She had to stop frequently and lean against a wall or a lamp post when a contraction swept over her, and for a few seconds afterwards she would breathe deeply, her forehead broken out in sweat. No one saw this agonisingly slow odyssey down the grey, mist-covered streets, a fact for which Carrie was thoroughly grateful.

Mrs Jones lived above her grocery store in a small apartment, and she answered the door in her curlers and a bathrobe, her eyes widening when she saw who was leaning on the doorbell.

'Good heavens!' she exclaimed at the sight of Carrie's white face.

'The baby's coming,' Carrie said faintly, and crumpled on the doorstep.

She only had vague memories of the events that followed; being carried to a car and brought into the small local hospital, the physical examination and the urgent voices over her head, the trolley that sped her to the delivery room or the struggle by the resident doctor and local pediatrician to save the baby girl that was born fifteen minutes later.

She slept for hours, sedated and watched over by a concerned nursing staff. When she finally awoke, it was to find the sun setting, a thin beam of light coming through the curtain in her room. She turned in her bed and saw a hazy figure standing before the window.

'Alex?' she asked, her voice weak.

'No.' The hazy figure moved over to her bed, and Carrie saw that it was a plump woman with a kindly face in the white uniform of a nurse. A cool hand touched her forehead. 'How are you feeling?'

Carrie tried to think, her mind drowsy and disorientated. 'Dizzy,' she said at last.

'That's to be expected. Let me wind the bed up a bit for you.'

She was in a small room, Carrie saw, and her bed had metal bars that were raised on both sides. She was covered by a white sheet and when she shifted slightly, she could feel that the gown she was wearing was open at the back.

'This is a hospital,' she said.

'Yes, dear.' The nurse plumped her pillows, rearranged her sheet and pressed a buzzer over her bed.

Memories of the night before swept over her in a flood of frightening images. 'The baby!'

The nurse wouldn't let her sit up, but gently pressed

her back against the bed. 'The doctor will be here in a minute.'

Carrie was suddenly frantic. 'Please,' she begged. 'Is the baby all right?'

The nurse was saved from answering when the door opened and the doctor walked in. He was a short man with white hair and horn-rimmed glasses over shrewd brown eyes. Carrie was never to forget his face or the way he sat beside her and took her cold hand between his warm ones.

'How are you feeling, Mrs Moore?'

'The baby,' she said urgently. 'Is it . . .?'

'She didn't live,' he said gently. 'We tried to keep her alive, but she was too premature.'

Carrie didn't answer, but turned her head away and stared dry-eyed at the opposite wall.

'We're not exactly sure why you went into such an early labour,' he continued, 'but it happens sometimes. It means that you'll have to be watched carefully during your next pregnancy, but it doesn't mean that you won't be able to have fine, healthy children at some later date.'

Carrie continued to stare blindly at the geometric design on the wallpaper opposite her bed, and the doctor sighed. 'We'd like to contact your husband, Mrs Moore.'

'He's . . . out of the country.'

The doctor and nurse exchanged glances. 'Is there anyone we could call for you?'

Carrie shook her head vehemently.

'There's a Mrs Jones who would like to see you. Shall I let her come in?'

Carrie shook her head again. 'No,' she whispered. 'I'll see her when I go home.' She didn't think that she could bear to see Mrs Jones. Her only wish at the moment was to get the doctor and the nurse out of the room so that she could cry in peace.

'Fine.' The doctor patted her hand once more and stood up, giving a signal to the nurse, who left. 'But I'd like to keep you here for a few more days before discharging you. Just for observation.'

Carrie nodded. 'All right,' she said dully.

'Good,' he said, his smile professional. 'I'll be back tomorrow morning for a visit.'

The tears were not cathartic; they didn't ease the heavy burden that lay on her chest like a permanently attached weight or an aching sense of loss that made every emotion she had felt in the past seem trivial in comparison. Over the next few days, as her body recovered, Carrie came to understand how very happy her life had been until the moment she had lost the baby. She had been protected in an insular little world, quite divorced from trauma or catastrophe. Her grandparents were still alive and healthy; her parents were vigorous. Death had not been a part of her existence; it had only been a shadow on the horizon, like a far-away storm whose sounds were muted and whose threat too distant to matter.

The edge of her grief was so sharp and unbearable that Carrie wondered how people survived the death of those they had loved and held. She had never even seen her baby and only held it in the cradle of her body. In some ways she was thankful that she did not have a face to remember or the feeling of a small body in her arms, but she did mourn the child that she had never known; the one who had moved within her and whose face she had imagined in her dreams.

Despite the efforts of the doctor and nursing staff, Carrie was lethargic and depressed, a condition complicated by the usual post-partum emotional upheavals. They kept her in the hospital as long as they could, only discharging her with reluctance. Carrie never knew that the doctor had conferred with Mrs Jones and that his warning about her mental state was grave. Nor did she recognise Mrs Jones' concern or Mr Finch's worry. It wasn't like her, but Carrie was oblivious to those around her, accepting their anxious visits and troubled enquiries with a dull lack of interest.

She walked for long distances on the beach, finding that the angry winter ocean suited her mood. She brought bread along for the rapacious gulls and watched them catch the scraps in mid-air, swooping down with an elegant grace. She concentrated on the feel of the cold wind on her face and the stinging spray of the water on her skin, throwing off her hood so that the elements could beat against her, believing that their harshness kept her mind off the deeper pain. It wasn't until months later that Carrie would understand how much she had wished to hurt herself in the weeks following the baby's death. She blamed her own body for that premature labour. The baby had been healthy and strong; she was the one who had failed.

Carrie told Mrs Jones and Mr Finch the same story that she had told the doctor, saying that her husband had gone out of the country and, because of the way he was travelling, was unable to be reached. She assured them that she was fine and didn't need anyone, insisting that Mrs Jones should not phone Veronica in New York on her behalf. 'She's far too busy with the company,' Carrie said. 'I don't want to bother her.'

November turned to December, and the last month of the year brought a day-long snowstorm. The beach house wasn't that well insulated, and Carrie found that its rooms were chilly. She took to wearing her heavy sweater and gloves on her hands to keep her fingers from freezing. The snow swirled around the beach house, covering the front steps and blowing in through the screens to cover the porch floor with a shifting carpet of white. Carrie pulled on her windbreaker and a pair of boots and, after digging out the steps, walked to the beach where she watched the snow blow into the raging, grey waves, the sun a pale yellow smudge in the overcast sky. When she returned to the house, she found that the drifts had covered the steps, filling in the trench she had dug out. Nature, she thought bitterly, had a way of obliterating any evidence of life as if it had never existed.

She stamped her feet against the mat on the porch and opened the front door. A waft of warm air touched her face and she looked into the kitchen with surprise. She saw that the oven door was open and the electric coil within was a deep red. 'Hello!' she called out, expecting that Mr Finch had come over.

'I was wondering where you were,' a deep voice spoke.

'Out walking,' Carrie said evenly, discovering to her surprise that not even Alex's presence had the power to rouse her from her apathy. 'I didn't see your car.'

He stood up from the kitchen chair, watching her carefully. 'I couldn't get down the street—too much snow.'

Carrie didn't answer, but pulled off her boots, leaving them side by side next to the front door. She hung her heavy slicker on a hook and wiped the snow off her hair. She hadn't even bothered to comb it that morning and the long honey-brown strands were tangled down her back. Her cheeks were flushed from her walk, but she didn't look healthy. Her skin was pale, dark shadows lay beneath her eyes and she was thin to the point of emaciation. Not that she cared about her appearance. Carrie had long since stopped looking at her image in the mirror.

'Would you like some coffee?' she asked, walking around Alex and filling the kettle with water.

'That would be nice.'

She put the kettle on the stove, aware of his eyes on her back, but not caring about his perusal. She knew that she looked sloppy and unattractive. The jeans she wore were baggy, and her black sweater had a hole on the shoulder and its surface was pilled beyond repair. 'Do you take milk and sugar?' she asked.

'Just black, thank you.'

The mugs didn't match. One said *The Manhattan Ballet keeps New Yorkers on their toes* and the other had a picture of a crowing rooster on it. She filled them both with coffee and set them down the kitchen table, her hands steady and competent. Alex picked up the ballet cup and smiled at the words. 'Very clever,' he said.

'It was Bonnie's idea,' Carrie responded, sitting down at the other side of the table and sipping at her coffee. She noted, with detachment and indifference, that Alex looked tired, that his dark hair curled damply on his forehead, that his dark blue Nordic sweater suited his colouring and that his lean fingers were clenching the mug until his knuckles had turned white.

'She told me that you lost the baby,' he said slowly.

Carrie felt a stirring of interest. 'How did . . . ?'

'Veronica told her.'

'Oh.' Carrie could clearly see the chain of events. Mrs Jones had gone back on her word and called Veronica; the ballerina had told Bonnie; and her room-mate had confided in Alex. Why not? After all, they were lovers.

'I also ran into Casimir Rudenko at a party recently.'

'Did you?' Carrie was suddenly breathless, brought out of her lethargy with a snap. There was something in Alex's eyes, something frightening.

'I accused him of being callous and selfish.'

'I don't suppose he liked that,' she said, her mouth dry.

'No, he didn't know what the hell I was talking about.'

Carrie frantically sought for an explanation. 'He didn't know about the baby! I told you that I didn't tell . . .'

A muscle leapt in Alex's jaw. 'I know what you told me, but I thought he was a real bastard not to have tracked you down. If you'd been lovers, the least he could have done was find out where you were and how you were feeling.'

'I didn't want . . .'

'But, surprise! You weren't lovers. Or that's what he told me.'

Carrie tried a weak smile. 'Casimir has slept with the whole company.'

'Except you,' Alex said grimly, 'a fact that he apparently intends to remedy.'

Carrie looked intently down into the steaming liquid into her cup as if she could decipher the future in its dark depths.

'You lied to me,' he continued, his voice low but no less threatening.

She saw no reason to prolong the lie. The baby was dead; nothing mattered any more. 'I . . . had to.'

'Why?!'

The fury in his voice made her flinch. 'I . . .'

'Why didn't you want me to know that it was mine?' His fist hit the table so that the coffee spilled from her cup. 'Why?'

Carrie looked up, appalled at the anger that twisted his mouth into a hard slant. 'Because I was afraid of you,' she stammered.

Alex's dark brows pulled together. 'Afraid?'

'Afraid that you'd insist we get married or that you'd want the baby.' She shook her head in confusion. 'I thought I'd be safer if you didn't know. It was my life, after all, not yours.'

'Didn't you think that it was my child, too? That I would want to know?' There was a bleak despair in his voice, but how could Carrie tell him that she had never forgotten, not for one single second, that he was the father of her child?

'I'm sorry,' was all she could say.

'Sorry!' Alex spat out the word as if it were a disgusting morsel of food. 'Sorry!' he repeated, standing up from the table, his fists clenched.

'What else can I say?' she asked tiredly. 'Anyway, it's over.'

There was a long silence. Carrie sensed Alex standing there, staring at her bent head. Finally he sat down again and asked in a defeated tone, 'How long did it live?'

'Only for a few hours.' The words were painful for her to say. She hated to think of the way her baby had struggled for life.

'Was it a boy or a girl?'

She glanced up at him in surprise, wondering why he cared. 'A girl.'

'Why did it happen?'

'Why did what happen?'

'Why was she born so early?'

Carrie looked away and took a deep breath. 'I went into premature labour. The doctors don't know why exactly.'

'But it wasn't the baby,' he insisted.

'No!' she flared at him, suddenly furious. 'It wasn't your goddamned genes at fault! You can sleep easier tonight.'

'Carrie . . .'

'It was me—do you understand? Not the baby. She was . . . perfect!' Tears sprang into her eyes.

Alex's face softened. 'I never . . .'

The front door slammed. 'Hello?' a voice called out. 'Carrie? I came to check on that darned furnace. It's older than the hills and goes on the blink every now and then.' Mr Finch appeared in the kitchen door, bundled up in an ancient leather jacket and a cap with flaps that covered his ears. He started to speak again, but stopped, glancing uncertainly from Carrie's drawn face to Alex.

Carrie stood up quickly. 'Come in,' she said, trying to smile. 'Alex, this is Mr Finch, my next-door neighbour. Mr Finch, this is Alex.'

'Pleased to meetchya.' Mr Finch pulled off his glove and held out a gnarled hand. 'And I'm real glad you came. Your wife's been looking a bit peaked lately.'

Alex threw Carrie a look that made her shrivel, but when he shook Mr Finch's hand, his expression was bland and pleasant. 'Has she?' he asked smoothly.

Mr Finch pulled off his cap and ran his fingers through his shock of white hair. 'Ever since she lost the baby . . .'

'Coffee, Mr Finch?' Carrie asked hastily.

'No, thanks.' He turned again to Alex and Carrie saw with resignation that the old man was going to persist and right what he perceived as a grievous wrong. 'It was a big shock to her, a big shock, and she sure ain't been eating well, I can tell you that.'

Alex raised an eyebrow. 'I couldn't agree with you more,' he said. 'I thought she looked thin.'

'And she's damned lucky she ain't caught pneumonia, 'cause she's out there on the beach for hours.'

Alex got into the act with a vengeance. 'Carrie,' he said in a scolding voice, 'you have to watch your health.' He reached out with his hand and, caressing her cheek, added in a falsely solicitous voice, 'I don't want you sick.'

Carrie glared at him before giving Mr Finch a sweet smile. 'Coffee?' she asked again.

'No. I won't keep you folks.'

She put out a restraining hand. 'Alex was just leaving to go back to New York, Mr Finch, and I'd really appreciate it if you did take a look at the furnace.'

'Well,' he said hesitantly, looking from one to the other, 'if Mr Moore is about to go . . .'

'He is,' Carrie said firmly, and turned to Alex, 'aren't you . . . darling?'

Their glances locked and the battle was fought silently as Mr Finch took off his coat and hung it over the back of a chair. Carrie prayed fervently that Alex would leave.

She could see the dark glint of anger in his eyes, and she felt far too tired to cope with any further argument. She was, as she had said, sorry that she hadn't told Alex about the baby, but she no longer wanted to talk about it. The birth and death were a part of her life that she wanted to put in a box, cover with a lid and bury deep into the past.

'But . . . darling, if you aren't feeling well, you should come back with me,' Alex protested, and Carrie's hands itched to wring his neck.

'He has a point there, Carrie. The weather here ain't going to get much better.'

She looked from one face to the other. Mr Finch's was earnest; he was completely fooled by their charade. Alex's, on the other hand, showed nothing more than husbandly concern. Only his dark eyes revealed the anger beneath his façade. 'I'm not ready to face the city yet,' she said, lighting with relief on a plausible excuse.

Mr Finch nodded his head gravely. 'I can see that,' he said. 'I ain't never been partial to the city in my life. This is as close as I'll ever get.'

Carrie gave Alex a pleading look. 'I'll come home soon.'

'I can't leave you for too long,' Alex replied with a sincerity that would have passed muster on the Shakespearean stage. 'I'll be back on the weekend.'

'Gotta check up on the little woman now and then,' Mr Finch agreed, nodding his head with an air of masculine camaraderie that made Carrie's teeth grate together. It was quite obvious that the old man had seen Alex, judged him and given him a stamp of approval.

'That's right,' Alex agreed silkily. 'It was nice meeting you, Mr Finch. Keep an eye on Carrie for me.'

The old man looked pleased at the responsibility. 'No problem,' he said, pouring coffee into a mug.

Alex turned to Carrie. 'Walk me to the door . . . darling?'

There was nothing she could do but follow him into the hallway where he pulled on his coat. 'Goodbye, *Mrs Moore*,' he said sarcastically.

'I never used you as an excuse,' Carrie hissed in a furious whisper. 'He just assumed that you were my husband.'

'But it was convenient,' Alex retorted harshly, his eyes resting on the gold band that adorned the third finger of her left hand.

'All right,' she said tiredly, 'I didn't want my neighbours to think of me as an unmarried mother.'

'Then you won't mind if I exercise my husbandly prerogative.'

'What husbandly . . . ?'

'This,' he said, bending his dark head.

The embrace and kiss held no gentleness or tenderness; it was strictly an exploitation of her mouth and her body. His hand ran in an impersonal fashion over her skin; his lips moved brutally against hers. Alex was acting in cold blood, and Carrie shivered under his touch, recognising it as a kiss of frustration and anger from a man who had been duped, lied to and used. In a way, she couldn't blame him; in a way, she felt that she deserved to be punished, and when his hand moved under her sweater to her unrestrained breast, kneading her soft flesh, she remained passive beneath his rough exploration.

Alex lifted his head and gazed down at her. 'No response, *Mrs Moore*?' he said mockingly. 'I can remember when you could barely wait until I got you into bed!'

'That was a long time ago.'

'It could happen again.'

'Never!'

His smile held no amusement as he pushed open the front door. 'Never is a long time,' he said, his voice filled with a threat. 'We'll see how long you can make it last.'

An overwhelming fatigue drove Carrie into bed that night long before her accustomed time, and she slept until lunch. When she got up, the snow had stopped, but a bitter wind made the windowpanes rattle in their frames. She ate a quick sandwich and then went back to bed again, sleeping until midnight, when she roused enough to visit the bathroom and eat again before falling back into bed, her eyelids heavy and weighted. It was as if Alex's visit had broken the back of her insomnia. She had slept poorly after the baby's death, often dreaming, often waking at frequent intervals. Now, it seemed that her body was fulfilling a sleep obligation of enormous proportions and she simply couldn't keep awake, her mind and body seeking that grey oblivion where she didn't dream and didn't think, where everything was erased and pain didn't exist.

The following morning, the house was cold and she couldn't start the oven, but the thought of dressing to call on Mr Finch was too exhausting, and Carrie simply piled more blankets on her bed and went to sleep again with a pair of gloves on her hands and a woollen cap on her head. When Veronica arrived, she found the front door blown open, a glass of milk on the kitchen table frozen solid and Carrie buried under a mound of blankets, coats and sweaters.

'Carrie! Wake up!' Veronica shook her hard.

'Go away,' Carrie groaned.

'Up!' Veronica commanded. 'Right now!'

Carrie forced her eyes open and stared into the other woman's concerned face. 'I'm too tired to get up.'

'Nonsense! It's past three o'clock and from the looks of it, you've been sleeping for days!'

'It's too cold,' Carrie protested.

'I just got the furnace going and I fixed the stove. There's coffee on, and you're going to drink it.'

'Just a short nap,' Carrie pleaded, her eyes closing again.

Veronica tore off the blankets and pulled her upright. 'It's a sign of depression.'

'What is?'

'Sleeping like this. Now, I want you up, washed and in the kitchen in five minutes.'

Carrie yawned and rubbed her eyes. 'Why didn't you join the Army, Veronica? You missed your vocation.'

'I prefer to practise on you. Now, come on—up!'

Carrie groaned but got up. In the bathroom mirror, she saw a sight that made her grimace. Her hair was tangled around her head and her eyes were gummed from sleep. She washed her face, brushed her teeth and attempted to comb her hair, wincing at the knots and unhappily noticing the way its former lustre had dimmed to a dull brown. She had let herself go after the baby's death; her looks hadn't seemed important, but now she cringed when she thought of the way Alex had seen her and she understood the look of disbelief in Veronica's eyes. She'd never been the kind of woman who spent all her spare time improving on nature, but she had always been fastidious.

'That's better,' Veronica announced when Carrie arrived in the kitchen, dressed in a clean blouse and jeans, her hair braided into a single plait.

'I'm sorry,' said Carrie, 'I didn't give you much of a welcome.'

Veronica set a plate of warm stew in front of her and a cup of steaming hot coffee. 'Eat,' she ordered. 'You look terrible!'

Carrie obediently ate, drank and cleaned her plate to Veronica's satisfaction. 'Now,' said Veronica as she put the plates in the sink, 'tell me about the baby.'

Carrie looked down at her hands. 'There's nothing to tell.'

'But I want to know.' Veronica sat down beside her, compassion in her dark eyes. 'I want to know everything.'

So Carrie told her everything from beginning to end. From meeting Alex in Florida to their argument two days earlier. From the discovery of her pregnancy to that horrible moment in the hospital when she had found out that the baby hadn't survived. From the strong feelings of love she had had for her unborn child to the oppressive burden of her grief. When she was done, Veronica sat silently for a second, then shook her head. 'It's time to go on living,' she said.

'For what?' Carrie asked.

'For your career, if nothing else.'

'I have no career.'

Veronica frowned. 'Of course you do.'

'I'm out of shape—badly.'

Veronica snapped her fingers. 'I can remedy that in a month if you're willing to work,' she said, then added shrewdly, 'What about Alex?'

'What about him?' Carrie asked evasively.

'You don't care about this man who fathered your child?'

It was hard to lie under Veronica's dark, honest gaze. 'I . . . I'm not sure.'

'Perhaps your feelings run more deeply than you imagine?'

'It doesn't matter if they do. He's going out with Bonnie.'

'Ah,' Veronica said softly. 'I've met him, then. A tall man with black hair? Very good-looking and charming?'

'Charming?' Carrie asked bitterly. 'You must be kidding!'

Veronica merely smiled. 'You think he's having an affair with Bonnie?'

Carrie shrugged her shoulders helplessly. 'Bonnie attracts men.'

'Does she know that he was the father?'

'No.' Carrie gave Veronica an intent look. 'And don't

tell her, please. What's past is past, and I don't want to interfere in her relationship with Alex.'

'I think you're foolish,' Veronica said vehemently.

Carrie was surprised at her intensity. 'Foolish?'

'If I were you, I'd never give up a man I cared for without a fight.'

There was something in her voice that made Carrie look at her in wonder and try to imagine what kind of lover Veronica had been. She had once been beautiful, and by anyone's standard could still be considered as handsome. She was lithe and slender, her features were well defined, her head regal with its coronet of greying braids. If Veronica had ever been in love, it would have been an affair of passion and strong emotion; she never did anything by halves. Carrie wondered what had happened in Veronica's past that she had now chosen to be celibate. As far as Carrie knew, or anyone else for that matter, the older woman lived alone and preferred it that way.

'But I don't want to fight Bonnie,' she protested.

'Bonnie is flirtatious and unstable,' Veronica said flatly. 'She goes through men the way Sherman marched through Georgia. Even if she does have her claws into your Alex, then I can't see it as anything other than temporary. She'll be bored in no time.'

'It would be difficult to go back,' Carrie explained with a sigh when she thought about living with Bonnie and the endless hours she would have to spend at the barre forcing her body back into its dancer's shape.

'Yes,' Veronica agreed. 'Very hard, but you can do it.'

Carrie gave a wry laugh. 'I'm glad you have faith!'

'I watched you in the corps, and five years ago I told myself that you would be my successor. I saw you coming and I could feel my crown tremble on my head.'

'Oh, Veronica, I never meant to . . .'

Veronica raised an imperious hand. 'That's the way the world works. The young replace the old, and it happens more quickly in ballet than anywhere else. You're a fool to give up what you now have to immerse yourself in an endless cycle of grief. Mourn, child, but mourn while you dance. It will give you extra power and depth.'

'*No experience is wasted*,' Carrie quoted a Gregory aphorism.

'He's right. Any adolescent can acquire technique, but it takes maturity and experience to make a dancer.'

Carrie sighed at the enormity of the task Veronica had set before her. She saw nothing but pain ahead, physically and mentally. She knew what was involved in the arduous task of strengthening muscles grown weak from lack of use, and she didn't know if she were capable of watching Bonnie dress for a date with Alex or listening to her talk about a night they had spent together. She foresaw that the ache of her body would be nothing compared to the sharp pangs of her jealousy. 'I don't know if I can go back,' she said at last.

Veronica gave her a shrewd glance. 'You've had it far too easy, Carrie.'

'Easy?' Carrie gave the older woman a look as if she were mad. What had been easy? Her career with its awesome hours of work? Her relationship to Alex? The loss of her baby?

'I'm not crazy,' Veronica said calmly. 'You've never had to struggle. You grew up in a comfortable middle-class home with parents who squired you from one ballet class to the next. You had enough native talent to rise quickly, and your drive and ambition accomplished the rest. You even got the man you wanted within an evening of meeting him!'

'But I didn't want . . .'

'You wanted him, child. Face it—you wanted Alex the moment you saw him, and I would say you haven't lost him yet. No man keeps visiting a woman that he doesn't care about.'

'He was only interested in the baby,' Carrie said dully.

Veronica ignored her. 'And now that you're finally facing a really difficult task, you're sleeping your life away.'

Carrie wavered. 'Perhaps I need more time.'

Veronica slapped the table with a force that made her flinch. 'Time is the one thing you don't have,' she said angrily. 'You're an absolute fool if you think so. You were on your way to being one of the country's finest dancers, and you can still get there if you come back.'

It wasn't the dream of being the country's finest dancer that stopped Carrie from objecting further. She'd long ago learned how frightening success could be, because the other side of the coin was failure, and she could fall into the abyss with one false step. No, it was the meaning behind Veronica's words that stopped her. In all the time that she had trained under the older woman's strict tutelage, she had never received such high praise. Veronica had scolded her and driven her almost beyond endurance, but only very rarely had she given her a nod of approval. This compliment that Veronica was paying her meant more to Carrie than praise from any other quarter. Her family was always supportive; the critics were as fickle as a summer storm; and Gregory had been a one-man cheering squad since the day she had joined the company. But Veronica was her mentor, a dancer, a peer who understood the exact value of everything Carrie had accomplished.

'Do you think so?' she whispered in bemusement.

'Carrie,' Veronica said softly, her dark eyes intent, 'come back with me. I will make you a dancer again.'

CHAPTER SEVEN

HER return to New York and the world of ballet was infinitely more difficult than Carrie had ever envisaged. Despite the good will of her fellow dancers and their earnest advice, she discovered that there was no easy route back to her earlier strength and flexibility. She was stiff from lack of exercise and her turn-out, the movement which allowed a dancer to turn knee and foot to the side, was almost completely gone. She trained eight hours a day, taking classes with the most advanced group in the ballet school as well as daily classes with the company. She trained until every muscle from her neck down rebelled against the constant stretching, moving and twisting.

She came home every day, weary and aching, soaked in a hot bath, ate a quick dinner and then collapsed into bed. Nothing seemed to matter except for the moments when she danced and could feel herself regaining the supple line and smooth grace that had been her hallmark. Later, when she would look back on this period of her life, Carrie would remember it as a film that moved too quickly, the images blurring into one another. Christmas and New Year came and went, barely rippling the surface of her life. She developed callouses on her hands from gripping the barre and bleeding blisters on her feet from her pointe shoes, but she also began to lose the soft flesh around her abdomen that had been left after her pregnancy, and the muscles on her legs grew ever more defined.

The press conference on her return was an ordeal, but otherwise everyone was kind. She received a happy letter from her parents and a warm, understanding note from Julie. She found a bouquet of flowers before her locker, a present from the corps de ballet. Gregory brought his jacket along to wrap around her shoulders after a class was over, saying that he didn't want her to catch a cold. Veronica made an appointment with her own personal masseuse, and Bonnie kept the press at arm's length, issuing reports that Carrie was back in training but not yet ready for a performance. The little touches and small personal favours, she found, buoyed her up when the going got rough and she felt like forgetting that she had ever been a ballerina or thought she could be one again.

In a way she found that the physical training was not as arduous as the mental discipline it required. Grief was an emotion that could not be set aside; it crept up on her unawares, hitting her at odd moments. She might be having coffee with someone when she would suddenly think of the baby, or in the middle of a rehearsal or travelling home on the bus. Then the sense of loss would envelop her like a dismal grey cloud, and she would lose her ability to concentrate on what she had been doing. Sometimes tears came, other times she would just turn pale and start to tremble. Those closest to her came to recognise the symptoms and would sympathetically turn aside until the moment passed. She categorically refused to talk about the baby to anyone, even Bonnie, who lavished tender loving care on her and an unfailing concern for her welfare.

Casimir had become, as Bonnie had told her, a semi-permanent fixture in the apartment, usually arriving for dinner on weekdays and visiting on weekends. He was overjoyed at Carrie's return, appalled at her appearance, and effusive about his determination to have her back on the stage. To her surprise, Carrie found that she looked forward to his company.

'You must eat, *lapushka*,' he said one night as he bustled around the kitchen making dinner. He often arrived with a bag of groceries or a container of home-made soup or stew, being disdainful of what Carrie and Bonnie ate and the way they stocked their refrigerator. 'Good Russian food that makes the blood move in your bones.' He rolled the R in Russian with satisfying exaggeration.

'Veins,' Carrie corrected him. 'Blood moves in veins.' She was seated on a stool by the counter watching him deftly chop up cabbage.

Casimir shrugged. 'You must have food that builds your muscles. I am tired of dancing with that bean.'

'Bean?' she queried.

'Marion. She is so skinny; I think her bones will cut my hands.'

'String bean,' Carrie said with a smile. 'When a person is thin, we call him a string bean.'

'And she is no dancer,' Casimir assured her with an emphatic twirl of his knife.

'I thought Marion was doing well.'

'Not like you, *milaya*. Not like you.' He gave her the Casimir smile, the one designed to melt a woman's heart like ice under sun, and Carrie couldn't help smiling back, despite her fatigue. He wore a pink apron over his jeans and sweatshirt, a lock of blond hair fell across his broad forehead and his blue eyes were caressing. Carrie had discovered that being around Casimir was like taking an invigorating tonic. He was buoyant, vibrant and carefree, and his aura of good health seemed to enfold her when he was near.

'My God! What concoction are you making now?' Bonnie had arrived home and was standing in the doorway of the kitchen, her nose wrinkling in disgust.

'Good Russian borscht,' Casimir replied as he dumped a handful of cabbage into the large pot of beet soup. 'The way my mother made it.'

'Now, why couldn't you have defected from France?' Bonnie sighed as she put her handbag down on the table and wearily took off her coat. 'That way we'd have gourmet meals instead of peasant's fare.'

Casimir shook a finger in her face. 'The Russian peasant was strong.'

'Like a mule,' Bonnie agreed sarcastically, 'and just about as smart.'

He feigned reproach. 'You would insult my countrymen?'

'Darling,' Bonnie drawled, 'if they're all like you . . .'

Casimir gave Carrie a blasé look. 'She is jealous of my good Russian stock!'

Bonnie gave up the battle and sat down by Carrie. 'What a day!' she said with a groan. 'I had an irate patron on the phone for two hours this afternoon. He wants front row seats for the gala in April and can't understand why his thousand-dollar contribution doesn't entitle him to red carpet service.'

Casimir and Carrie both eyed her sympathetically. The fight for seats and perks was always a difficult one. Front seats and access to backstage were given out according to the size of a patron's contribution, and a thousand dollars was not very large in comparison to some. The Manhattan Ballet Company was funded not only by individuals but by corporations who usually gave large donations. One of those companies had decided to fly in a President and a Board of Directors for the gala, and Carrie knew that they had already been given the choicest seats in the house.

Casimir handed Bonnie a thick slice of pumpernickel bread. 'What do I do with this?' she asked, turning it over in her hand with a look of distaste.

'Eat it.'

'Plain?'

'No butter; it's not good. You're not looking so well, Bonnie. Too many late nights?' He leered at her in a friendly fashion.

'Now who's jealous?' Bonnie said calmly, as she bit into the bread. 'Or are you preparing to enter a monastery? Really, Casimir, your reputation is on the skids. The corps is taking bets to see how long you can last without sex!'

They bantered, exchanging friendly insults and outrages, neither taking the other too seriously. Carrie smiled as she watched them, but she noticed for the first time that Casimir was right about Bonnie: she didn't look well. There was nothing that Carrie could put her finger on; Bonnie was, as always, well dressed and immaculately made up, but she seemed weary and her flirting with Casimir lacked its customary zest. It was, Carrie thought, as if her glitter had dulled, her sparkle dimmed by some concern or worry.

She ticked off every aspect of Bonnie's life and couldn't come up with one flaw. Other than irate patrons, her job was challenging; her family was healthy and happy; and her love life seemed quite satisfactory. As far as Carrie could ascertain, Alex phoned her frequently and they often went out to dinner after Bonnie left work. Carrie had no idea when Bonnie arrived home from these dates; nothing could rouse her from sleep and she was utterly thankful for the fatigue which held her in such deep slumber. She really didn't want to know about Bonnie's relationship with Alex. The details, she thought, would kill her.

Jealousy, she had found, was almost as insidious as grief. It was there, lying in wait to attack when she least expected it. The sight of a couple entwined on a park bench could make her heart feel as if it were breaking; certain strains of music brought tears to her eyes. She chided herself for being a romantic fool and for believing that she was hopelessly in love. She tried to think of love as a sickness, a disease that could be cured by time, forcing herself to consider her celibate nights as doses of medicine and hoping against hope that the more she was alone the less lonely she would feel. But there was, she discovered, no remedy for what ailed her, and she spent

a good deal of her days and all her nights with the painful
sensation that she was incomplete, as if an integral part
of her were missing.

Veronica had said that she should fight for the man
that she loved, but Carrie couldn't even find a battle-
field. She hadn't seen Alex since her return, and she
guessed he was avoiding her. His last words to her in the
beach house had suggested that her indifference was a
challenge to him, but she suspected that once he had
cooled off, he would discover that he no longer cared if
she responded to him or if he ever saw her again. Her
presence would only remind him that she had lied to him
and about him. She couldn't blame him for the way he
felt; she had treated him badly and she knew it.

She threw herself with greater urgency into her dancing, but nothing could stop the quick catch of her breath
at the sight of a pair of broad shoulders and a dark head
or the sudden racing of her heart if she heard a voice that
resembled his. There were times when she came close to
hating Bonnie, and it was an emotion that she tried to
push away, knowing that Bonnie was innocent, unaware
that Alex had been in Florida, was the father of Carrie's
baby and the man she loved. Carrie felt as if she were
caught in an unholy triangle and, in a desperate attempt
to extricate herself, she began to go out with Casimir.

To her surprise their dates were as innocent as that of
two lambs enclosed in the same pasture. They did the
sort of things dancers do to release tension, going to the
movies and attending informal gatherings where the
conversation revolved around dance gossip and shop
talk. Casimir, as usual, dominated at these parties,
talking and gesturing and laughing with the same fervent
gusto that he brought to his dancing. He would often
throw his arm around Carrie as he talked in a friendly
sort of way. Their pairing was noticed by everyone, and
since it differed so much from Casimir's usual intense
romanticism, the gossip about him took a new turn.

Carrie caught its edges: they were, it was rumoured, *very* serious about one another, Casimir had settled down, wedding bells would ring in the not so distant future.

She laughed about the gossip to herself, acknowledging that only one part of it was true. Casimir, it seemed, had settled down. He was certainly different from what Carrie had expected. She had anticipated fighting him off at every turn, but he was gentle, considerate and completely asexual. She wasn't sure of the cause, but she assumed that, like everyone else in the ballet company, he believed she had suffered from a nervous breakdown and required time to recover. She was grateful for his newly-developed thoughtfulness, but she couldn't help being suspicious that the old Casimir would return in full force when she least expected it, and she was careful to be with him only when other people were around.

One night they went with a group of other dancers to a nightclub, an elegant establishment that catered to New York's élite. It was a special occasion because they were celebrating a birthday of one ballerina, an anniversary for a married pair and the recent promotion of a male dancer to principal status. Carrie wore an ivory silk dress with criss-crossed straps and a swirling skirt and let her hair hang loose in honey-brown waves down her back. As was customary at times like this, the group was boisterous, loud and thoroughly enjoying themselves. There were many toasts and a lot of jokes and laughter. Carrie relaxed and enjoyed herself, leaning against Casimir's shoulder and smiling at whoever was speaking.

By the end of the meal, their table was littered with empty bottles of champagne, and Carrie, usually abstemious, was feeling the effects of drinking more than she was accustomed. Her head felt light and she had a tendency to find everything extremely amusing. She was laughing heartily at a remark, when she chanced to glance around at a table newly occupied by a group of well-dressed men and women and found

Alex's dark eyes resting on her.

She turned away quickly, her feeling of being light-headed now compounded by a leaping forward of her pulse and a chill that made goosebumps raise on her arms.

'Cold?' asked Casimir, tucking his arm around her even tighter.

But she wasn't cold any more. The chill had now been replaced by a sensation of heat that was making a flush rise up the back of her neck, and she felt as if the lacy black shawl she was wearing over her backless dress was suffocating her. But she didn't shake off Casimir's arm; on the contrary, she moved closer to him as if he could protect her from that cold glance.

The lights went down as the nightclub act started and Carrie was forced to sit through a comedian that she didn't find funny, although Casimir and the others were roaring, and a singer who was ultimately forgettable. When the acts were over and the music began for dancing, she tried to suggest that they leave, but everyone looked at her as if she'd lost her mind.

'This is fun dancing, remember?' one dancer teased her. 'No pliés!'

'Casimir, I'm a bit tired and . . .'

'I want to dance with you, *lapushka*. I'm tired of that bean Marion.'

He dragged her on to the small dance floor in front of the band and swept her into his arms, revolving her around with enthusiasm. Carrie avoided looking in Alex's direction, but she was convinced that he was watching them. She felt a certain tension in the air despite the laughter and low hum of the people surrounding her. It was as if a storm crackled in the distance, charging the atmosphere with pent-up electricity.

'Hmm, I like dancing with you, my American *milaya*. I am going to tell Gregory that you are ready for a new pas de deux. It is time for us to perform again.' He nuzzled her neck.

'Casimir!' she protested, pulling away from him.

'I will be Romeo to your Juliet.' He nibbled on her ear.

'Please!'

'Siegfried to your Odette.' He licked his tongue on her lips.

Carrie turned her head frantically, realising with dismay that the old amorous Casimir had returned like a bad penny. 'Stop it!' she said sharply. 'You know I don't like . . .'

'May I cut in?' Alex stood there, tall and lean in a dark suit, his black hair combed back, his cheeks lean and well shaven.

Casimir glanced from Alex, whom he recognised with a frown, to Carrie, standing frozen in place. 'Well, *lubimaya*?' he growled.

Carrie didn't want an argument in public. 'It's all right,' she said, touching his arm. 'Go dance with Pamela; she's all alone.'

She sounded so assured that Casimir complied, but she was trembling, and Alex felt it as soon as he took her in his arms. 'I make you nervous, don't I?' he asked.

'I . . . was worried about Casimir,' she replied evasively.

'He gets jealous?'

'Frantically,' she said, wondering why she felt it so necessary to lie to Alex whenever she saw him. There were no links between them any more now that the baby was gone, and she certainly didn't need a fictitious relationship with Casimir to protect her from him, but the feel of his arms around her on a dance floor brought back disturbing memories and Carrie automatically fought the emotions they evoked.

Alex gave her a dark, enigmatic look. 'Has he achieved his goal?'

'What goal?'

'To get you into his bed.'

'I hardly think it's any of your business,' Carrie said hotly.

'Call it curiosity,' he said silkily. 'I'm always interested in what happens to old girl-friends.'

'Then I'm afraid that your curiosity will have to remain unsatisfied. I don't discuss my love life with strangers.'

A light flared in the dark depths of his eyes. 'I don't think I'd call us strangers.'

The music stopped then, and Carrie thought she would be able to escape, but Alex insisted upon bringing her back to his table and introducing her to the people who had accompanied him. As she had noticed earlier, they were all obviously well-to-do, the men in finely tailored suits, the women glittering with jewels, their dresses sophisticated and elegant. Several of them had seen her dance and were effusive with their compliments. It was a situation that Carrie was used to; she replied with modesty, signed an autograph for a woman's daughter, 'Twelve and a budding ballerina!' and talked with one knowledgeable man about the recent trends in modern dance. But all the while, her mind was on the woman who was standing by Alex. She had straight auburn hair that hung to her white shoulders, slanted emerald eyes, a flawless complexion, a low-cut black dress and diamonds at her ears, neck and fingers.

'We've met, Miss Moore,' Leona Sole said. 'Backstage in San Francisco.'

'Yes,' said Carrie, 'I remember.' She didn't think she would ever forget the night that Alex had seen her dance, and she particularly remembered the woman who had introduced him to ballet. Now she wondered how long Leona Sole was staying in New York, and whether Bonnie's air of malaise had anything to do with her arrival.

'But you haven't been dancing since then, have you?' Leona asked with an almost malicious curiosity.

Carrie was aware of Alex's watchful gaze. 'No, I was exhausted after the tour and took several months off.'

The green eyes couldn't have been more limpid or innocent when Leona spoke. 'I'd heard that you were pregnant.'

Carrie stiffened, but kept her face impassive. 'Really? It's amazing how off-centre the gossip mill can get!'

With a tinkling laugh, Leona turned to Alex. 'You know Daddy's connections, darling. He heard it from . . .'

'Miss Moore doesn't look pregnant to me,' Alex interjected smoothly. 'On the contrary, she looks extremely fit.'

Did his remark reflect the way she had looked last time Alex had seen her, with her hair in dirty tangles and her eyes lined and shadowed? 'I've recovered,' Carrie said pointedly. 'I'm dancing again.'

His mouth twisted. 'With dedication, no doubt.'

Leona wove a shapely arm through his. 'Darling, all dancers are dedicated, aren't they, Miss Moore?'

'Very,' said Carrie, knowing that Alex was marking her words and reading between the lines. He knew what she was saying; that she'd turned back to her career, that she was determined to succeed and that, by doing so, she had made a choice about her life.

'Don't you ever wish for something different, Miss Moore?' His voice was seemingly laced with an idle curiosity. 'A husband, children, a family to grow old with?'

Carrie cringed inwardly at his cruelty. How could he ask her that before all these people and, in particular, the woman who was hanging so intimately on his arm as if he belonged to her, as if she were one of his lovers?

'No,' she said coldly, her amber eyes raised defiantly to his. 'I used to, but I don't any more. A husband would be a hindrance; children would get in the way.'

'You see, Alex,' said Leona with a careless shrug of her bare shoulders, 'a man would be a fool to get involved with a ballet dancer. He'd play second fiddle to her career.'

Perhaps the idea came from seeing Alex again, or perhaps it simply arose from the depths of despair into which she had fallen. Carrie would never know where the ballet came from, only that it came almost full-blown into her mind, three scenes and stunning choreography for the whole company. It was about a man and his woman and child; it was about revenge and murder and loss. Carrie mulled it over in her mind for several weeks before writing it down and showing it to anyone. She had, in the past, occasionally choreographed a little dance, a short routine or two, but never a complete ballet, and her own audacity astonished her. But she was introspective enough to realise that she had created this ballet for the sole purpose of being in it. As in the past, she yearned to work out her emotions as she danced and the ballet, as she envisaged it, would allow her to dance out the unhappiness within her.

Veronica heard the idea first, gave Carrie a shrewd look and suggested that she collaborate on it with Gregory. He had, she said, the experience and the know-how to put it together. Gregory, in his usual ebullient way, was enthusiastic and showed it to the Board of Directors. Within a couple of weeks, the go-ahead was given and Carrie, who was used to being at the rehearsal end of a ballet, found herself enmeshed in the details of creating one. She and Gregory hashed and rehashed the story line, wrangling over every idea to make sure it worked. It had begun as a simple plot about a husband who murders his child in a fit of anger and is sent to jail, leaving his wife to mourn both the loss of her man and her baby, but as they worked on the different sections of the ballet, it developed into a far more complex and dramatic story. Another man was added, a casual flirtation, a husband's jealousy, a carnival scene.

They tried out the ballet in a workshop, amending and changing it as the dancers threw in other ideas. Carrie worked on her own part, spending hours alone in the studio, dancing that scene when the child is murdered over and over, until she dropped from exhaustion, her black leotard damp from sweat, the satin tips worn off her pointe shoes. The Board decided to premiere the ballet, now entitled *Revenge Motif*, at the gala performance, and the work intensified. Costumes had to be designed, dancers chosen, the sets made.

Bonnie finally caught Carrie at the studio as they passed in the hallway. 'It's publicity time,' she said. 'I need about an hour with you. I've considered sending you a telegram, but I'm not even sure that Western Union could find you.'

Carrie gave her a rueful grin. 'Has it been that bad?'

'Baby, I haven't seen you in weeks. Literally!'

Carrie knew that she was right. They might have been living in two separate apartments for all the times they had actually seen one another. Carrie was up and gone in the morning before Bonnie was awake and their evening schedules rarely matched. She no longer had any real idea whether Bonnie was going out with Alex or not. Not that she really wanted to know. She preferred to remain in ignorance; it hurt less that way.

'I have a meeting with Gregory right now.'

'Can you come by my office in about an hour?'

Carrie nodded and rushed off. She always seemed to be racing somewhere, but beneath the frenetic pace of her days lay the knowledge that she was vainly trying to relieve the gaping, painful emptiness of her life with action: any kind of action. Thinking required time, and she was filling up every second of her day with meetings and rehearsals. Veronica had accurately predicted that she would need a month to get back in shape, and now that Carrie was no longer fighting her body every step of the way, she could concentrate on dancing itself, the only way she knew of curing herself of a sadness that was expressed in restless energy and sleepless nights.

The ballet, *Revenge Motif*, consumed her. It was the vehicle for her return to the dance world and just might be, she once confided in Gregory ruefully, her swan song. She could not deny to herself that it was the hardest thing she had ever done, not the steps themselves, but the concept of the ballet as a whole. It touched upon her so deeply; its emotions flowing from her own experiences, and she wondered whether she would be able to dance the story before an audience, displaying the very rawness of her wounds, the very well-spring of her soul.

Casimir both helped and hindered her. They were finally dancing together again and he was, she thought, magnificent in the part of the husband. But he hadn't restricted his flirtatiousness to the evening in the nightclub, and Carrie found that she was having trouble holding him at arm's length. He would murmur sweet nothings in her ear, nuzzle her at the slightest opportunity and beg her to go to bed with him. He never left her alone if he could help it—which was why she was so surprised to pass him in the hallway as she walked to Bonnie's office and realise that he had not even noticed that she was there. He was scowling ferociously, his broad forehead in a frown, red colour high on his cheeks, one side seemingly more red than the other. Carrie stopped and stared as he marched by, watching the angry set of his shoulders, muscular and bare beneath the straps of his brown leotard, and wondered what or who had made him so furious.

She found Bonnie standing by her desk, smoothing down her hair and drumming her fingers on the blotter.

'Did you and Casimir just have a battle?' asked Carrie as she flopped down in a chair.

'That . . . that oaf thinks he's God's gift to women!'

'Made a pass at you, did he?' Carrie asked with a smile. Bonnie was one of the few people in the company who knew that she and Casimir were not a 'couple.'

Bonnie sat down angrily, her face still flushed. 'That would have been easy to live with,' she said sarcastically. 'No, he sat here and discussed the women in his life. What the hell does he think I am? A confessional?'

'You mean he named them?'

'He not only named them, he discussed their salient features, one by one. I now know more about the corps than I ever wanted to know!'

Carrie wondered at the intensity of Bonnie's disgust. She was usually able to handle men with aplomb and could take even the most off-colour joke with equanimity. 'Maybe he needs to brag a little,' she said mildly. 'He's not getting anywhere with me.'

Bonnie gave a brittle laugh. 'You mean he hasn't tried to impress you with his list of conquests?'

'I think I know them already.'

'He's really quite . . . impossible!'

Carrie gave her a curious glance, guessing that Bonnie was not telling her all that had passed. The deep red mark on Casimir's cheek suggested that he had been quite emphatically slapped, and Bonnie wasn't the type of woman who hit a man on a flimsy pretext. 'You two really mix like oil and water.'

'Actually, we ignite,' Bonnie said ruefully. 'We're inflammable.'

'Perhaps there's a bit of an attraction between the two of you?' Carrie hazarded.

Bonnie gave her an astonished look. 'Don't be ridiculous!'

'Well, he is sexy. Even I can see that.'

'Sexiness requires more than a pair of biceps, a handsome face and a pair of wandering hands,' Bonnie retorted forcefully.

The question trembled on Carrie's lips while she fought against her own aroused curiosity. She sensed that she would regret asking, but she found that she could no longer couldn't resist knowing the truth, no matter what pain she would later suffer. She took a deep breath like a diver about to plunge into cold, icy depths. 'Like Alex?' she asked.

Bonnie looked down at the file on her desk as if to shutter the expression in her eyes. 'Alex is very sexy,' she replied.

'Oh.' Carrie paused. 'Then you are seeing one another.'

'Did you think that we'd split up?'

Carrie retreated hastily. 'No, I just wondered . . . I mean, you and I haven't had much chance to talk lately and . . .'

'Alex and I see a lot of one another.'

Carrie could barely swallow. 'Is . . . it serious?'

Bonnie gave a nonchalant shrug. 'Maybe,' she said, and picked up the file. 'Now, about this new ballet. The press is going to want to know if . . .'

Carrie could barely listen as Bonnie waded through clippings and discussed publicity. Her mind was whirling with the implications of Bonnie's statement. She had never known her room-mate to even be remotely serious about a man, and even her casual 'maybe' indicated that her relationship with Alex went deeper than any other that she had had. Carrie didn't dare to dwell on what that 'maybe' actually meant. She knew that Bonnie wasn't the least bit squeamish about sex, and she could only guess that they had been sleeping together for months already. The thought of Bonnie and Alex entwined on a bed made her feel physically sick.

'Are you feeling all right?' Bonnie glanced up from the sheaf of papers in front of her and gave Carrie a concerned look.

'I'm . . . fine. You were saying about the costume designs . . . ?'

Bonnie bit the end of her pen. 'They're so gorgeous that I thought we might leak a picture or two to the press and . . .'

When she thought about it, Carrie could only see that
Alex and Bonnie were right for one another. They were
both urbane and sophisticated; they both belonged to
the glittering world of wealth and power. Alex had said
that he only travelled by choice, and Carrie imagined
that once he decided to settle down, his job would be an
élite one. A wife like Bonnie would be a tremendous
asset to him; she already knew all the right people and
had the right connections. Carrie had lived long enough
with Bonnie to know the kind of lifestyle that accompanied that sort of money and acquaintances. As a
couple, they would think nothing of owning an elegantly
decorated penthouse in Manhattan, a casually luxurious beach house in the Hamptons and a pied-à-terre in
Paris. There would be catered cocktail parties and
dinners, tennis tournaments and yacht regattas . . .

'I swear, Carrie, you haven't heard a word I've said.'
Bonnie gave her an impatient frown.

Carrie came to with a jolt. 'Woolgathering—I'm
sorry.'

'Now, listen, because this is very important. The
dance critic for the *New York Times* called yesterday
and . . .'

Carrie suddenly remembered Leona Sole, and her
own unhappiness was shot through with a furious burst
of loyalty to Bonnie. The other woman had hung on
Alex's arm as if he were a possession, her green eyes
caressing him with the sort of emotion that was reserved
for lovers. If Bonnie and Alex had reached the point of
commitment, the arrival of Leona must have caused
Bonnie a great deal of pain. It was no wonder that her
room-mate hadn't been herself lately, and Carrie put
aside her own feelings as she identified with Bonnie's
anguish; jealousy was an emotion with which she was
well acquainted.

Now that she took the time to notice, she could see

how drawn Bonnie appeared. Underneath the make-up, there were circles beneath her eyes and lines running between her mouth and nose. Her blonde hair was in its usual smart cut and her pale green silk dress had an haute couture design, but Bonnie looked as if she weren't sleeping well, and Carrie reproached herself for not being more observant and with being immersed and obsessed with her own miseries. After she had lost the baby, Bonnie had been kindness itself, and the least Carrie could do was let her know that she understood and offer her sympathy and help.

'I saw Leona Sole with Alex,' she began hesitantly. 'About a month ago in . . .'

Bonnie threw her an astonished glance. 'Whatever are you talking about?'

Carrie leaned forward and said softly, 'I ran into Alex in a nightclub, and he was with Leona Sole. Bonnie, I'm not sure that you have to worry about her, because she lives in San Francisco and . . .'

'I know all about Leona Sole,' Bonnie said with exasperation.

Carrie sat up straight. 'You do?'

'God, yes. They were lovers about four years ago.'

There was a certain kind of news that had the painful power to take Carrie's breath away. She knew about Alex's previous women; he hadn't hidden them from her, but that didn't mean that she liked meeting a former mistress or having her nose rubbed in the fact of their intimacy. But she pushed away her own feelings, determined to help Bonnie with her problems. 'But when I saw them,' Carrie said reluctantly, 'she acted as if it had never ended.'

'That's because Alex called it off.'

'Then why were they together?'

Bonnie was blasé. 'Because Alex and Leona's father do business together.'

'But doesn't it bother you that he's with her?' Carrie exclaimed.

Bonnie opened her mouth as if to say something, and then paused, looking away from Carrie and down at her hands. 'Alex and I have an understanding,' she said coldly.

Carrie knew when she had been rebuffed. 'Oh,' she said, unable to keep the hurt out of her voice.

Bonnie looked up, contrite. 'Look, I can't quite explain it to you right now, but . . .'

Carrie shook her head quickly. 'It's all right, you don't have to explain anything to me.'

For a second, Bonnie seemed to lose her accustomed poise. 'This isn't my choice, baby. I don't mean to . . .'

Carrie stood up. 'Please, Bonnie, I shouldn't have interfered. What you do with Alex is strictly your business. I just . . . hope you'll be happy.' And she left the room in a hurry because she could feel the tears stinging behind her lids, and she didn't want to cry before the woman who had an 'understanding' with the man she loved. It was evident that Bonnie wasn't unhappy at all, at least not about Alex or Leona, and that in fact she had her life sewn up quite nicely. Carrie couldn't help being happy for her; she wanted the best for Bonnie, she really did. She just couldn't help fervently wishing that her friend's well-being didn't rest on her own misfortune.

She made it to the rehearsal without crying and threw herself into work with a vengeance. It was the scene that she danced with the corps de ballet, a carnival scene where she runs among the merrymakers looking for her husband, knowing that murder is on his mind. The different dancers, dressed in masked costumes, grab her and force her to participate in their revelry while she frantically tries to elude their attention. Carrie surpassed herself, causing even Veronica to acknowledge her skill and technique, but she knew that her intensity didn't come from the ballet. She was running from her own thoughts, struggling to escape from her own life, her own desperation masked in the dance.

CHAPTER EIGHT

THE knowledge that Bonnie and Alex were on the road to matrimony led Carrie to accept a date with Casimir that was quite different from anything they had done in the past. They had usually gone out with the dancers' crowd, but this was a special occasion—her twenty-third birthday—and Casimir wanted to celebrate it alone with her at a restaurant known for its high-priced gourmet meals and equally high-class clientele. It was an elegant place, almost church-like with long stained-glass windows and high carved ceilings. The table linen was a fine ivory damask; the cutlery was sterling and the plates that they ate off were a bone china with a gold band.

Carrie knew that they were recognised by the formally clad maître d' and his army of deferential waiters, but everyone had far too much good taste to acknowledge their celebrity status. Besides, when she had entered the restaurant, Carrie had noticed a famous actress, a well-known musician and a businessman whose latest corporate take-over had graced the front page of the *New York Times* for several days. She didn't often go out to such places; the prices were high and the food far too rich by a dancer's standards, but on the rare occasion that she did, Carrie made sure that she enjoyed herself.

They had a privately situated table in a corner that was shielded by a luxuriant fern, and their meal involved several waiters who flambéed filet mignon before their eyes and set the dessert aglow in blue and green cognac flames. Casimir was attentive without being overly demonstrative, and Carrie thought he looked quite superb in a dark blue suit that barely confined the muscular dimensions of his body, his fair hair slicked back and the

light gleaming along the edge of his high, Slavic cheekbones.

He talked about growing up in Russia and his begin-
nings at the Kirov Ballet. Carrie had never known the
full story of his background or how poor his family had
been, or the effort it had taken for him to defect. He
laughed when he talked about it, but she sensed an
underlying nostalgia and thought that no matter how
long Casimir lived in the United States, he would never
be quite at home. His family had remained behind in
Russia, and he hadn't seen them or heard from them
since his arrival; there were cultural and ethnic links to
his fatherland that tied him inextricably to his past.
Carrie wondered whether Casimir was lonely beneath
his façade of bubbling confidence and bonhomie.

Their conversation turned to her childhood and her
ambitions, and Casimir listened to her with an unexpected interest. Carrie found herself talking about a
future in choreography, a topic which had lain quietly at
the back of her mind but had never been voiced before.
The dancing life of a ballerina was so short, she told him,
and she wasn't sure that she was cut out to be a teacher
like Veronica. They discussed the problems of mounting
new works in an era where less and less money was being
allocated to the arts, and Carrie discovered that Casimir
was surprisingly knowledgeable about the business
aspects of running a company. There was a peaceful
harmony between them by the time they returned to
Carrie's apartment, and she invited him in for an after-
dinner drink, unwilling to end the evening and face her
own thoughts.

'To your birthday,' he said, lifting his narrow liqueur
glass. They were sitting side by side on the velvet couch,
watching the flames leap high in the fireplace. The heavy
gold curtains had been drawn across the full-length
windows and the living room had an air of serene
isolation. The noise from the street below was subdued,

and there was little sound beyond the murmur of their voices and the crackling of the fire.

'It's been a nice one,' she said with a replete sigh, stretching her legs and curling her stockinged toes in the carpet. She was wearing a soft wool dress in cherry red that had tiny fabric-covered buttons running up to a square neckline and long sleeves whose fullness was reflected in the soft gathers of the gusseted skirt. Her hair was up in its dancer's chignon and her amber eyes looked huge in their fringe of thick, dark lashes.

Casimir reached over and idly began to pull the pins out of her hair. 'On my last birthday, I got drunk on vodka.'

Carrie laughed. 'I remember—you were awful!'

'Awful? How can anyone be awful who is marvellously drunk on good Russian vodka?'

Carrie leaned back against the sofa and Casimir's arm. He had taken off his jacket and tie and she could feel the warmth of his skin against her neck. 'I don't know how you can drink the stuff,' she admitted. 'I think it tastes like medicine.'

Casimir leisurely unwound the long swathe of her hair and let it hang over his arm in a shimmering dark-gold curtain. 'You have to be Russian, *milaya*, to appreciate vodka.'

The fire hissed and spat, sending tiny red-gold sparks on to the hearth where they gleamed briefly against the dark tiles. Carrie closed her eyes and snuggled into the curve of Casimir's arm. He was, she thought drowsily, comfortable to be with when he wasn't trying to impress a crowd or being the centre of attention. And gentle as well. She barely felt the caress of his hand on her hair or noticed when it moved to the curve of her cheek. She was sleepy and warm and surprisingly content. She didn't have the heart or the energy to object when his lips met hers, and her mouth opened willingly under his.

It was a pleasant kiss, and Carrie responded to it,

letting Casimir explore her mouth and the feel of her shoulders through the wool of her dress. His arms tightened around her; his thumb moved in warm circles on her throat. His mouth moved from her lips to an earlobe and then back to her mouth again, this time with more intensity. Carrie was acquiescent under the slow pace of his lovemaking and willing, even eager, to see if another man than Alex could arouse her. She lifted her arms around Casimir's neck, feeling the coarse strands of his hair with her fingers. He was virile and handsome, and she wanted desperately to be in love with him, to grow weak with that passionate languor that Alex was able to create in her by his slightest touch.

But within minutes she had to concede defeat, and when Casimir stopped kissing her, his mouth moving to her throat where he had unbuttoned her dress, Carrie sighed and he lifted his head, regarding her with a brooding look.

'This isn't working,' he said.

She shook her head. 'I'm sorry.'

Casimir sat back and muttered an imprecation in Russian. 'I must be losing my touch,' he said, growling.

She patted him on the arm. 'I like you very much,' she said soothingly, 'but I don't think we can be any more than friends.'

He gave her a sideways glance. 'You don't mind?'

'I'd hoped there would be more,' she said honestly, knowing that she had gone out with Casimir in the hope of diverting her emotions away from Alex and trying in vain to break the ties of that earlier attraction. 'In some ways, we'd be an ideal couple.'

He caressed her cheek with his finger. '*Lubimaya*,' he said sadly, 'we were never meant for one another. It is not written on the moon.'

Carrie's correction was automatic. 'The stars,' she said. 'Written in the stars.'

Casimir leaned back and stretched, his broad chest

straining against the thin fabric of his shirt. 'I too had hoped for more. Perhaps I'm used to making passes at you.'

Carrie smiled at him. It was odd to think of Casimir as a creature of habit. 'You haven't been too happy lately, have you?' It was more a statement than a question. She had sensed his moroseness when they danced together. His flirtatiousness had seemed thin and forced as if he were concealing an underlying unhappiness.

Casimir gave her a rueful glance. 'I'm as obvious as the nose on my face?'

She curled her legs up under her. 'I've wondered,' she said. 'You used to take out the girls in the corps so fast that I couldn't keep count, but then you stopped as if you didn't care any more. It wasn't like you.'

'I got bored.'

'I thought maybe . . .' She paused, unwilling to express a suspicion that had been growing in the back of her mind for some time. 'Well, I just wondered if you weren't interested in Bonnie.'

Casimir groaned and threw out his arms in a dramatic gesture. 'I've fallen for her . . . flat!'

Somehow Carrie wasn't surprised at all. 'Just fallen,' she said. 'Not flat.'

'Flat, round, over, under, you name it. She is driving me crazy, that woman. Absolutely crazy! Can you imagine me, Casimir Rudenko, in love with a woman who doesn't give a damn?'

'Oh, I'm sure she likes you,' Carrie objected.

'Like!' Casimir spat out the word in theatrical disgust. 'I don't want her to *like* me! I gave up other women for her. I die for her and she doesn't even know I'm alive!'

It was hard not to smile, but Carrie managed. 'Why haven't you told her that you . . . ?'

Casimir was working himself into a frenzy. 'Tell her? I told her. I said that I was a fool in love for her, and all she did was slap my face and call me a philo . . . phila . . .'

'Philanderer.'

'And who is she to talk? You know the reputation of that woman? That she goes through men the way I drink vodka.' Carrie couldn't deny Casimir's accusation, so she just shook her head in sympathy. 'So I try to make her jealous by going out with . . .' He suddenly gave Carrie a guilty look.

'It's all right,' she said, 'but I'm afraid it hasn't worked.'

Casimir looked morose. 'I know. She goes out with that Alex, the man who danced with you at the night club.'

Carrie looked down at her entwined fingers so that Casimir would not see the dismay in her eyes. It would seem that everyone knew that Alex and Bonnie were serious about one another. 'Yes.'

He glanced at her lowered eyes and the unhappy twist of her mouth. 'You are in love with him?' he asked gently.

She nodded.

There was a long silence as they both stared into the depths of the fire as if the glowing coals and leaping flames could yield up a solution to their entwined problem. Carrie was far too unhappy to see the situation in anything other than a bitterly ironic manner, reflecting without humour that her life could have been the basis for a Shakespeare play. She and Casimir were a fine pair of star-crossed lovers!

Casimir's thoughts, it seemed, had taken a similar turn and then gone one step farther. '*Lapushka*,' he said in a serious voice, sitting up and rolling up the sleeves of his shirt, 'do you know what this calls for?'

Carrie shook her head. 'What?'

'Vodka,' he said, slamming one fist into the other. 'Good, strong Russian vodka!'

*

Casimir got stinking drunk. There wasn't anything Carrie could do about it. He had brought a bottle of vodka over some weeks before and no one had opened it. Casimir did it justice—more than justice, if the truth be known. He drank the whole thing while Carrie watched in horror, her own glass empty because she refused to participate. He went from being morose to garrulous to a stupor, and at the end, he lay prostrate on the couch, snoring. Carrie covered him with blankets and almost wished she could indulge in something as cathartic as vodka. As he had poured in the liquor, Casimir had poured out his heart. It would seem that he had fallen for Bonnie months ago and she had broken his large Russian heart several times over.

Casimir couldn't understand why he loved her and he had bemoaned his fate loudly and volubly, but Carrie saw that he and Bonnie had a lot in common. They were both fun-loving, vivacious and full of boundless energy. Even their attitudes toward the opposite sex were similar. Until he had fallen in love, Casimir had regarded women as wonderful toys, designed solely for his pleasure and gratification. Bonnie's view of men was a little more complicated, but she basically saw the opposite sex as exploitable. Carrie wasn't surprised that Casimir had been attracted to Bonnie; she was, in a way, his alter ego and one of the biggest challenges he had ever come across.

Carrie bent over and clicked off the lamp by the couch, throwing Casimir's sleeping form into shadow. He was curved in the circle of cushions, and she hoped he didn't try to straighten in his sleep or he would have a rude awakening on the floor. She smiled at the thought, then realised that she had grown quite fond of Casimir. She didn't mind that he had used her to make Bonnie jealous. She deserved it; she had used him as a substitute for Alex. As she walked out of the living room, she decided that she was glad that they had come to terms and become friends. She knew how fiercely loyal Casimir could be, and . . .

The front door lock clicked, there was the sound of laughter, then the door itself swung open before Carrie had time to react. Alex and Bonnie sauntered in, laughing at some joke and looking, Carrie thought miserably, as if they were meant for one another.

They both had that elegant air that comes from money spent with no thought to cost. Bonnie wore a long silver sheath whose hem brushed against her silver sandals. Her dark ranch mink was buttoned up to her neck and a silvery-grey scarf was tied around her neck. Alex's fawn overcoat was unbuttoned, to reveal that he was in black tie and no less virile for the white frill of his shirt. It was the first time that Carrie had seen him in weeks, and if she thought that time had healed her wounds, she now discovered that she couldn't have been more mistaken. It made her ache just to look at him and to remember the way he had held her, the way his hard length had pressed against her. She felt a jolt when their glances crossed as if an arch of electricity had passed between them, a kinetic rush of energy that made her pulse start an erratic race, her heart beating in a rapid, breathless tempo.

'Did you have a nice evening?' she asked, her throat dry.

'Did you, darling? I think that's the question to ask,' said Bonnie, as she gave Carrie an incredulous look.

Carrie had quite forgotten what she looked like. Her hair was loose, flowing and tangled down her back, and her woollen dress was wrinkled from Casimir's lovemaking and her later struggles to make him comfortable on the couch. The top buttons of her bodice were open, the neckline falling away to reveal a glimpse of her lacy bra beneath. She kept her eyes on Bonnie, but she could feel Alex staring at her, his anger stormy and barely suppressed. 'Very nice,' she said, smoothing her skirt with nervous fingers. 'Casimir and I went out to dinner.'

There was a sudden mumbling from the living room and then an abrupt crash.

'What the hell—!' Alex exclaimed, while Bonnie rushed past Carrie into the living room.

When she switched on the lamp by the couch, they saw Casimir on the floor by the couch, holding on to his head, groaning and muttering in Russian. He wore no shirt; he had taken it off when he got into serious drinking, and the empty vodka bottle lay sideways on the coffee table, two glasses sitting beside it. Carrie couldn't help seeing how damaging it looked. She was in a state of dishevelment and Casimir was half-dressed. Even the most uninformed bystander would conclude that they had spent the evening drinking and making love.

Alex grabbed her arm as she tried to follow Bonnie. 'What's been going on here?'

Carrie felt as if his fingers would burn her. 'We were celebrating my birthday,' she explained.

Alex pulled her around to face him. 'You got drunk?' he asked in disgust.

Carrie lifted her chin. 'I'm not drunk.'

'No, but your boy-friend is plastered, and you look as if you've been manhandled.'

'It isn't what you think.'

'I think the worst,' he grated.

'You always have,' she retorted.

They glared at one another, his dark gaze burning into her amber ones, and Carrie wished desperately that she and Alex wouldn't fight when they met. It was as if they were wild animals with an instinct for the jugular. There had been times during her pregnancy when she had day-dreamed about having him as a husband, the baby gambolling at their feet. She could see now that it was quite ridiculous to imagine that they would ever have been compatible. Dislike and distrust ran between them like dark, uncrossable rivers.

'You . . . idiot!' Bonnie's exclamation forced their locked glance to break, and they both turned to find Casimir standing and holding her in a swaying embrace. 'You are the most uncouth man I've ever met!'

'What is uncouth?' he muttered, his lips on her neck. 'Is it English for I love you?'

'Don't be ridiculous!' Bonnie snapped, trying to extricate herself from his arms. 'I wouldn't love you if you were the last man on earth!'

They began to argue, passionately and loudly, and Carrie glanced at Alex, wondering why he was still standing beside her and not stepping in to protect Bonnie from Casimir's half-drunken, amorous passes. But it seemed that he was far more interested in her, because she found that he was looking down at her, the skin taut over his cheekbones, his mouth slanted in distaste. 'So this is your choice of lover,' he drawled.

'I can do as I please!'

'And also the father of your next child?'

Carrie was furious. 'Casimir loves children,' she retorted hotly.

'Are you implying that I don't?' Alex said, his voice soft but angry.

'All you cared about was the paternity of that baby,' she hissed.

A muscle leaped in his jaw. 'I wanted her as much as you did.'

'That's easy to say when she's dead!' Carrie had meant the words to be sharp and hurtful; she wanted Alex to feel how deeply her own pain cut, but once they were out of her mouth and hanging ominously in the air between them, she wished they'd never been said. A light of pure fury gleamed in Alex's dark eyes, the skin turned white around his mouth and nose.

'You little bitch!' he spat. 'If I could I'd . . .'

'Alex darling,' Bonnie called out, 'will you get take this drunken oaf down to the lobby and get him a taxi? I doubt if he could find his way out of a paper bag!'

Carrie slumped as Alex looked away, utterly thankful for Bonnie's intervention and Casimir's sudden revival. He had begun to sing a Russian song with loud enthusiasm, one arm slung over Bonnie's shoulder in a gesture of camaraderie. Alex had no choice but to go to Bonnie's aid, although he threw her one last furious glance before disengaging Casimir's arm from Bonnie's neck and leading him to the door.

'Call me tomorrow?' Bonnie asked as she opened the door for them.

Alex nodded, but Casimir took it as a personal invitation and reached out to caress Bonnie's cheek. 'Of course, *lapushka*,' he said thickly. 'I love you.'

Bonnie closed the door behind them and leaned against it with a weary groan. She was still in her fur coat, although the top button had been opened and her scarf pulled awry by Casimir's handling. She looked tired and drawn. 'What in God's name did you do to him?' she asked.

Carrie had just discovered that she was trembling and she put out a hand to the wall to prop herself up. 'I didn't mean to make Alex angry, but it seems that we can't see one another without . . .'

'Not Alex—Casimir. I've never seen him so drunk.'

'He decided to finish the vodka he brought us.'

'Finish it? It looks like he drank the whole thing; lock, stock and barrel!'

Carrie wasn't going to reveal Casimir's secrets, even if he had already blurted them out in his drunken state. 'He . . . was celebrating my birthday.'

'He's going to have a whopping hangover.' Bonnie leaned over and pulled off her high heels with a sigh. 'He's such an idiot,' she added, and Carrie could have sworn it was said in a tone of affection.

'He's a fine person,' Carrie said stoutly.

Bonnie yawned as she took off her coat. 'He might be

when he grows up,' she said. 'God, I'm exhausted! If I go to one more cocktail party like that, I think I'll die from sheer boredom!' She threw her coat over her arm and began to walk towards her bedroom.

Carrie touched her on the arm. 'I'm sorry about ruining your evening.'

Bonnie shrugged. 'You didn't ruin anything. I told you the party was awful.'

'I mean . . . about Alex.'

Bonnie had a strange look in her blue eyes. 'What about Alex?'

'He had to leave . . . take Casimir to a taxi . . . ,' Carrie stammered apologetically. 'He might have stayed longer if . . .'

Bonnie waved a hand negligently in the air. 'It doesn't matter.'

Carrie looked at her in surprise. 'It doesn't?' she asked.

'God, no,' Bonnie said airily. 'Alex and I have all the time in the world. Goodnight, baby.' And she walked away, leaving Carrie standing in the hallway, a lump thick in her throat as the truth of Bonnie's statement hit home. Of course, she and Alex had all the time in the world. When they were married, they would have hours of companionship and a lifetime of lovemaking. It was a thought that took Carrie's breath away, and she felt jealousy twist its knife inside her, cutting with an unexpected vehemence as if its blade had been whetted and honed to razor sharpness.

The gala approached with all the ominous intensity of a coming storm and the pace at the ballet studio became frantic. The dancers were gearing up for the performance, their nerves as taut as rubber bands on the verge of snapping. Rehearsals were marked by anger, tears and the occasional temper tantrum. The sewing room was in a frenzy when Carrie went down to try on her costumes and Mrs Martinelli muttered and mumbled through an entire fitting, her mouth bristling with pins. Bonnie was on the telephone constantly, and Gregory seemed to fly from room to room, despite his bulk. One of the few places that Carrie could find any calm was in Veronica's office, where the older woman presided in serenity, ignoring the whirling dervishes outside.

It was a tiny room at the end of a little-used corridor, but it had two windows and the benefit of the afternoon sun which streamed in through pale pink curtains giving the room a soft, luminous glow. Veronica had furnished it with a roll top desk of ancient vintage and two leather chairs. She had a small refrigerator and a hotplate under the window where she could steep pots of fragrant, aromatic herbal teas. Carrie would often visit her in the late afternoon when rehearsals were over and she felt in need of solace. Veronica had a way of putting the gala into perspective that Carrie appreciated. Everyone else in the ballet company acted as if the fate of the world rested on opening night, and it was refreshing to listen to Veronica's stories of other performances and their trials and tribulations.

'Did you see the rehearsal today?' Carrie asked one afternoon as she stirred a spoon of honey into her mug of tea.

'I had to teach at the school,' Veronica answered. 'Was it bad?'

'Gregory is going to succumb to apoplexy or heart failure, I'm not sure which,' Carrie said with a sigh.

Veronica leaned back in her chair. 'He's too excitable and he should take on an assistant. I've told him that a million times.'

Carrie nodded and idly twisted a loose pink ribbon on her pointe shoe. She was dressed in a typical dancer's rehearsal costume; an old brown leotard with one strap pinned together, pink tights with a long run down one leg and a pair of red and white striped leg-warmers. Her hair had fallen down during rehearsal and she had hastily pinned it back up into a lopsided chignon. Veronica, who came from an older school of discipline, by comparison looked elegant. She wore a long-sleeved black leotard and black tights with a short white tutu crisscrossed in front. Her hair was pulled back as tightly as it would go, not one strand out of place.

'Have you seen this?' asked Veronica, handing Carrie a newspaper clipping.

Carrie glanced at it and saw that it was part of a gossip column for a particularly sensationalist local tabloid. Under a picture of Bonnie and Alex coming out the doors of a hotel after a cocktail party was the caption, 'Socialite Bonnie Devitt Hughes has been seen frequently on the arm of eligible bachelor and tycoon, Alex Taylor. The grapevine is a-quiver with rumours of wedding bells and corporate mergers. Will the Hughes jet engine fortune be allied to Taylor's widely-held interests in oil and gas holdings? Tune in to this column for the latest developments.'

Carrie handed it back to Veronica. 'Ugh!' she said in disgust.

'Is it true?'

Carrie sipped at her tea. 'It would seem so.'

Veronica gave her a shrewd look, and she had the feeling that the surface of her nonchalance was as clear as glass and that the other woman could easily see the misery below. Grief and jealousy twisted through her in dark rivers of discontent. Although she still mourned the baby, her grief was not as strong as it had been; the emotion had a muted feel like the doleful tones of a faraway bell, its edge overshadowed by her unhappiness over Alex. She had sadly come to the conclusion that she wouldn't be able to live with Bonnie much longer and had made a promise to herself that she would start looking for another apartment after the gala was over.

'I was at that cocktail party,' said Veronica, pouring

herself another cup of tea. 'I don't think Bonnie and Alex are the slightest bit in love.'

Carrie fingered her mug. 'You don't?'

'I would say that they were friends, good ones, but not lovers.'

'Bonnie told me that they had an . . . understanding.'

'And what exactly does that mean?' Veronica said sharply.

Carrie looked up at her, surprised by the sarcasm in her voice. 'I don't know.'

Veronica leaned forward. 'Why don't you go and talk to Alex? Tell him how you feel and stop this nonsense?'

'Because . . . because I don't think he'd understand.'

'Understand what?'

Carrie chose her words carefully. 'How I feel about the baby. She was nothing to him, not really.'

'You don't think that he grieved for her?'

She shook her head. 'No.'

Veronica was silent for a minute as her forefinger traced the circular rim of her cup. 'Do you love him, Carrie?'

Carrie's voice was low. 'Yes.'

Veronica lowered her cup on to her desk with determination. 'Then I don't understand how you can let him go like this.'

'He's a free man,' Carrie protested. 'I can't stop him from going out with Bonnie!'

'I had a lover once,' Veronica said, 'And I lost him.'

Carrie looked into the other woman's face and suddenly saw how sadness had etched the deep lines from nose to mouth and the crease between her dark eyebrows. 'I'm sorry,' she said. 'I never knew . . .'

'But not to another woman, to cancer.' She ignored Carrie's exclamation of shock. 'It was worse than another woman, because his disease was with us every minute, the third person at our table and in our bed. I could never forget that it was there, but I fought it.'

Veronica clenched her teeth at the memory. 'I nursed him and I fought it and I wouldn't let him give in either. When he finally died, the doctor told me that Maurice had lived far longer than he'd ever expected.'

'Maurice . . . ?' Carrie asked, sitting up in sudden awe.

'Yes,' Veronica said grimly. 'Maurice de Launay was my lover.'

'I never knew,' Carrie whispered. Maurice de Launay was a legend, a dancer who had changed the course of ballet for men, giving previously stereotyped roles a level of sophistication and interpretation that had never been seen before. Carrie knew that Veronica had danced with him, but she had never guessed, even for a minute, that they were lovers. She tried to remember what she knew about Maurice de Launay. He had been married, of that she was sure, and she recalled reading that he had disappeared from the stage at the height of his career.

'He was only thirty-five,' Veronica went on as if she could read Carrie's thoughts. 'Far too young to die. He'd been estranged from his wife for years, so he came to me when he was sick and I hid him from the press. You'll never know, Carrie, how much I wanted him to live. If I could have breathed for him, I would have.'

Carrie made a murmur of sympathy, now understanding why Veronica lived alone and devoted her life to the company. There had never been a man in Veronica's life who had been Maurice de Launay's equal, and all the passion and tenderness that she had lavished on him had been switched to ballet.

'Don't you see why I'm urging you to fight for Alex?'

'What about my career?' Carrie cried in confusion. 'I can't have both, can I?'

Veronica sighed, her dark eyes filled with resignation. 'Your work will be sterile, child, if your life is empty. I learned that after Maurice died. That's why I think you're a fool if you give up the man you love.' She picked up the clipping and tore it into small pieces, letting them fall to the floor at her feet. 'And I don't believe this garbage.'

'I . . . wouldn't know what to say to him,' Carrie said, faltering. 'Whenever we're together we argue and fight. I . . . think he hates me.'

Veronica looked at her for a long minute, studying her slender face with its unhappy amber eyes and saddened, downturned mouth. 'Do you understand why you choreographed your ballet?' she asked.

'You told me that I should dance out my grief,' Carrie said slowly. 'I think the idea from the ballet came from that.'

Veronica nodded in agreement but went on, 'Have you ever wondered why you made the father guilty for the child's death?'

Carrie bit her lip. 'I . . . don't know. It seemed like a good story.'

'Yes,' said Veronica. 'When you dance that last scene, you're positively incandescent with hatred for Casimir. You're burning with anger.'

'I'm grieving,' Carrie objected.

'But your anger surpasses your grief, child. You're wonderful in your fury.'

Carrie turned the argument around. 'But the father deserves my anger. He murdered the child.'

Veronica gave her a smile. 'And the ballet reflects your life, doesn't it?'

'No!' Carrie exlaimed in shock. 'Alex had nothing to do with the baby's death!'

'Didn't he?'

'Of course not. He was there that day, but . . .' Her voice trailed off and then she swallowed, hard. 'Do you think that, subconsciously, I'm blaming Alex for being there that day and upsetting me?'

'Perhaps you blame him,' Veronica said, 'or perhaps

you're angry because he wasn't there when you needed him.'

'But I didn't want him,' Carrie objected. 'I never . . .' And then she paused when she remembered waking up in the hospital and hazily believing that the figure by her bed was Alex. It had, of course, only been the nurse, and she recalled with painful clarity the sharp stab of disappointment that had shot through her. Veronica was right: she *had* wanted Alex to be with her. She had longed for him all through the dark night of her labour, and when she found out that the baby had died . . .

'Of course you did,' Veronica said sympathetically, watching the pain on her face. 'He was the father of your child and you had every reason to want him there.' She took Carrie's hands between hers. 'He doesn't hate you, child; I suspect that he loves you deeply, but don't you understand what you've been doing to him? You've been hurting him for the sins he doesn't even know he's committed. Stop punishing him, Carrie, or he'll be lost to you for ever.'

CHAPTER NINE

THE day of the gala arrived, bringing with it all the mishaps appropriate to an opening night. The programmes were mislaid, one of the dancers fell sick and had to be replaced by a nervous understudy, and a costume ripped when it was taken off its hanger. The telephones were ringing off the hook and the hallways were in pandemonium. Carrie was compelled to attend an interview with Casimir on a morning television show and a news conference in the early afternoon. She barely had a moment to herself; there were a thousand details that seemed to require her attention, and she didn't escape from the studio until close to four o'clock. She had planned to go back to the apartment and wait for her parents who were flying in from San Francisco, but she had received a phone call from them in Chicago where their flight had been held up by thunderstorms. They were praying, they said, to make it to New York by the time the curtain went up. Carrie, dreading those long, empty hours before the performance, couldn't bear the idea of the apartment, so she went instead to the theatre where the gala would be held, knowing that no one would be there yet except for the doorman and a technician or two.

The theatre was dark and silent; her soft ballet slippers made no sound as she walked down the carpeted aisle to the stage. The curtain hadn't been lowered yet and she could see the set for the ballet, the pieces of furniture shadowy in the dim light. The first scene in *Revenge Motif* took place in the kitchen of an apartment, and Carrie liked the way the set designer had given the stage an air of domesticity. There were blue gingham

curtains on an imaginary window, a ring of pots and pans
hanging from the ceiling, and an old-fashioned wooden
cradle stood by a small table.

Carrie walked up on to the boards and walked around
the set, idly touching one prop and then the next. She
turned to face the dark auditorium, looking at the gold
and red velvet hangings on the boxes and then up to the
huge, gilt-covered chandeliers. It was a big theatre with
two balconies, and Carrie had often wondered what she
looked like to those who couldn't afford better seats and
sat up so high. She had learned to make her gestures
larger than life so that even the last row of the uppermost
balcony could see the movement of her hands, but
they would never be able to make out the expressions
of her face or the subtlety of line that made ballet an
art.

The theatre was so quiet that a pin dropping on the
stage would have made a clatter, and she made an
experimental pirouette, her loose dancer's skirt flowing
around her legs, the sound of her shoes brushing against
the floor. She stopped for a second to listen and then
moved again, this time slowly going through the steps of
the first scene where she said goodbye to Casimir as he
went to work and then circled the kitchen with the baby
in her arms. It was a scene of joy and contentment,
depicting her fulfilment as a wife and mother, and Carrie
danced it alone on the dark stage to an audience of mute
velvet chairs.

She could hear the music in her head, the sudden
deepening tones of the orchestra at the entrance of a
former lover, her shock, her refusal to go out with him,
his ominous insistence. She danced faster and faster,
imagining that Stephan Rains was beckoning to her. He
was a fine dancer and she thought that Gregory had done
well to choose him in the role of the other man. Stephan
was dark, lithe and exotic-looking; he was quite capable
of playing the devil if the part were assigned to him and

he was a good foil for Casimir, whose blond good looks were more muscular and masculine. Reluctantly, Carrie danced towards the imagined Stephan, the old lover who could still wield a sensual power over her. A *glissade*, then a turn, *pas de bourrée*, another *glissade*, then turn away; tiny frantic motions of her hands emphasising her despair. Yet she moved closer and closer as if she were being pulled by an invisible, powerful magnet.

A sudden clapping, isolated and loud in the empty theatre, stopped her in her tracks, and she peered into the dusky recesses of the auditorium, panting slightly from her exertion. 'Who is it?' she called out.

'Gregory.'

'Oh,' she said, relaxing. 'You scared me a bit.' Now she could see him, sitting in the fifth row. He was chomping on his cigar and his bald head picked up the light in its gleaming pate. 'What do you think?'

'It'll be a classic,' he said heartily.

'Since when are you such an optimist?' she teased.

Gregory's tone became serious. 'Since you decided to come back.'

'I'm so sorry,' she said, clasping her hands together. She knew how disappointed Gregory had been when she left, but he had never reproached her and had welcomed her back with open arms. It had never occurred to her that he looked to her for the success of the company.

'Well, listen, kid, I'm giving you a second chance to make good,' he said in a mock-growl.

Carrie laughed. 'I'll do my best.'

Gregory stood up. 'And make me a promise, will you?'

'Anything.'

'No more men. You know what men do to you. They ruin . . .'

'Your concentration,' Carrie finished for him in a dry tone.

'Good,' he said with finality. 'You got the message. See you later.'

Carrie watched his rotund shape as he walked up the aisle to the lobby and thought how appropriate Gregory's remark had been. What concentration she had left was in shreds and she clung on to every little bit in desperation, praying that when she was dancing she would forget about Alex.

She had mulled over Veronica's words, turning them over in her mind and examining every aspect until her head was spinning in confusion. She knew that she had fought off every overture Alex had ever made to her, both physically and verbally. She had fought desperately against his invasion of her privacy, believing that any knowledge of the baby would give him an unwelcome power over her. Yet even when the baby was dead, she had lied to him and said cruel things, her own harshness appalling her. Hate, it was said, was the other side of the coin to love, but Carrie had never before understood how entwined the two emotions could be. She was beginning to realise the way passion had woven itself through the very fibre of her being. She could never be impervious or passive to Alex; in his presence, she was either fire or ice.

Had she been punishing him unfairly, castigating him for not breaking through her carefully erected façade of dislike and indifference? When she looked back, Carrie could see quite plainly that Alex had tried, but she had fought his every effort tooth and nail. The more she thought about it, the more she realised that she had placed Alex in an impossible, no-win situation. He was damned if he did and damned if he didn't. She couldn't blame him for seeking solace in Bonnie's arms; she had driven him there, nourishing their affair by her own actions. Veronica had said that she didn't think they were in love, but Carrie wasn't sure she was right. There was more than enough evidence pointing in the opposite direction. Carrie saw no reason why Bonnie should lie to her about Alex.

With her shoulders drooping, both from fatigue and low spirits, she walked backstage to the dressing room that she had been assigned. It was a narrow room with a dressing table and a large mirror outlined with light bulbs on one wall and a sink in one corner. It was neither elegant nor glamorous, only utilitarian, and Carrie grimaced at the chipped porcelain of the sink and the long cracks in the dingy walls. Still, the room would be a quiet sanctuary for a few hours and she was in desperate need of peace. She put down the satchel which contained her make-up, leotards, tights and pointe shoes and curled up on a cot which stood against one wall, pulling a blanket over her. She needed to rest before the performance; she had been up since five o'clock that morning. She had to stop thinking about her love life, or the lack of it, and think about nothing but the ballet she would dance that night. Gregory was right, she thought as she wearily closed her eyes, men were murder on concentration.

'Wake up, baby!'

Carrie found Bonnie standing over her, shaking her by the shoulder. 'What time is it?' she asked groggily.

'Two hours before show time. No one knew where you were.'

'Are my parents here yet?'

'Nope. Rise and shine, star!'

Carrie sat up and rubbed her eyes. 'I didn't mean to sleep so long.'

'You probably needed it.' Bonnie sat down on the chair by the dressing table and, taking a tissue out of her handbag, blew her nose.

Carrie swung her legs over the edge of her bed and then stretched to reach her toes. 'I'm stiff,' she said, and then, hearing a hastily concealed sob, looked up in shocked concern. 'Bonnie! What's the matter?'

'I'm all r . . . oh, hell, the truth is that I'm miserable.'
Bonnie rubbed her nose with the tissue and gave Carrie a
watery smile. 'I'm ruining my make-up, too.' She was
dressed for the evening in a long black gown with a
sequined red and black bolero, and Carrie remembered
that the performance was being followed by a large
cocktail party in a nearby hotel. Bonnie had thoughtfully
brought her dress along, a shimmering blue silk, and
hung it on one of the pegs.

'Is it Alex?' Carrie asked hesitantly.

'No, Casimir. God, I can't believe I'm crying over that
man!' Bonnie exclaimed as she reached for another
tissue to dab at her eyes. 'He's making my mascara run!'

Carrie stared at her in alarm, horrible images coming
into her mind. 'What's happened to Casmir? Has he hurt
himself? Isn't he going to dance tonight?'

Bonnie gave a shaky sigh. 'Of course he's dancing
tonight. Why shouldn't he?'

'Then why . . .' Carrie suddenly stopped, her eyes
widening.

'That's it,' Bonnie admitted ruefully. 'I've fallen in
love with that uncouth, loud-mouthed, philandering
oaf.'

'But I thought . . . I mean, you said that you and
Alex . . .'

Bonnie shook her head. 'We're friends, that's all.'

'But . . .'

'I wanted to tell you long ago, but Alex had made me
promise that I wouldn't,' said Bonnie with remorse in
her voice. 'And then when you didn't seem to care one
way or the other, I didn't see what difference it would
make.'

Carrie looked at her in astonishment. 'Made you
promise what?'

'That I wouldn't tell you we were just friends.'

'But why?'

It was Bonnie's turn to look surprised. 'Baby, you

must know that Alex was very upset about the baby.'

'But he's in love with you!' Carrie faltered when Bonnie shook her head. 'He isn't? You mean that you and he were never . . . you were never attracted to Alex?'

Bonnie gave her a despairing glance. 'Baby, he's gorgeous! Of course I was attracted to him. What woman wouldn't be?'

Carrie was being very careful now, like a lawyer who had to pin a witness down thoroughly. 'Are you sure you're not in love with him?' she asked.

'Never. It was only a passing sort of attraction, and when I learned how he felt about you, that killed it.'

Carrie sat there, wide-eyed and stunned, relief rushing through her like a great wash of pure, clean water. 'Felt about me?' she echoed.

'Alex is crazy about you. He broke down and told me about it after you went to the Rockaways. Oh, I'll admit that I'd hoped to have an affair with him, but he confessed that dating me was the only way he could still keep in contact with you. He wanted to make you jealous, Carrie, that's what was behind all the secrecy.' Bonnie gave a low laugh. 'I told him it wasn't working; it was quite obvious that you didn't care about him at all, but he insisted.'

Carrie had never suspected that her act of indifference had been so successful. It had fooled everyone, even Bonnie. 'I don't believe it,' she whispered.

Bonnie leaned forward intently. 'I'm very fond of Alex. He's a good man, baby, and they're few and far between.'

'He didn't care about me,' Carrie insisted. 'It's his ego; I jilted him in Florida and then I lied to him about the baby.'

'You're wrong.' Bonnie shook her head emphatically. 'You hurt him, it's true, but it's you he wants.'

Carrie looked down at her hands, confused and

bewildered except for one thing. 'Wanting isn't enough,' she said quietly.

'Don't underrate the value of sex, Carrie. Platonic relationships are a dime a dozen; passionate ones aren't. Take Casimir, for example. I've never felt like this before and . . .' Her tears started again and she dabbed at them with a tissue. 'God, this is ridiculous! Every time I think of him, I turn into a fountain.'

'Why *are* you crying?' Carrie asked in bewilderment, thinking of Casimir's overtures to Bonnie.

'Because he's so damned unsuitable, and he reminds me of Mark, my first husband. Am I fated to fall in love with the same kind of man over and over?'

'I thought you and Mark didn't get along.'

'We didn't, and I suspect I was suffering from puppy love, but I had great hopes for that marriage, Carrie. Idealistic ones, I suppose; I was young then, but Mark put an end to any dreams that I had in no time.' Bonnie gave a bitter shrug. 'He went out with another woman on our wedding night!'

Carrie gasped in shock. 'You never said . . .'

'I never told anyone. It isn't the sort of thing a woman brags about.'

'And you think Casimir would do the same?'

Bonnie looked grim. 'His track record isn't spotless.'

'But he loves you,' Carrie said softly.

'So he says,' Bonnie replied mockingly.

'He's done everything to get your attention except stand on his head. He got drunk on my birthday because you'd broken his heart.'

Bonnie trumpeted into a tissue. 'I just can't envisage Casimir and me having a lasting relationship.'

Carrie gave her a smile. 'There's no harm in trying.'

Bonnie looked at her in surprise. 'Are you suggesting that we get married?'

'Maybe you both need to make a commitment.'

Bonnie gave a shaky laugh. 'The thought of it scares me to death!'

There was a knock on the door and another dancer poked her head inside. 'Carrie? Gregory wants to see you.'

'I'll be right there,' Carrie replied.

The door closed and Bonnie stood up, smoothing the long lines of her dress. 'I'm sorry about the deception with Alex,' she said, 'but I guess it doesn't really matter, considering the way you feel about him.'

Carrie gave her a wry smile. 'I'm in love with him, Bonnie. I've always been in love with him.'

Bonnie gave her an incredulous look. 'You're kidding! But . . . we must have made you miserable!'

'That's the understatement of the year!'

'Oh, Carrie,' Bonnie said softly, her blue eyes contrite, 'I'm so sorry. He loves you; I think he really does, because . . .'

The rapping on the door was insistent. 'Carrie! Gregory says he needs you immediately!'

'Coming,' Carrie called out, and headed for the door.

Bonnie put a restraining hand on Carrie's arm. 'Try not to think about it, please, until after the ballet. You can't afford to lose your . . .'

'Concentration,' Carrie finished drily. 'I know; I'm scared stiff!'

Carrie had no time to think about anything except ballet for the next three hours, but she danced with a lighter heart than she had had in a long time. Her loyalty to Bonnie had been like a ponderous anchor, holding her to silence and self-effacement, and she would never have tried, despite Veronica's advice, to steal Alex away from her. But now she felt as if the heavy weight of that tie was removed, leaving her buoyant and free. Bonnie's last words had given her an undeniable glow of anticipation deep inside. She was no longer so sure that Alex had continued to pursue her strictly to salvage his ego, and she dared to think that there might be a chance of a future for them. Hope lay within her; every dream springing again to life, but she shoved them away, knowing that nothing, not even happiness, must interfere with the ballet. Still, Alex was in the audience and there were moments that night when Carrie was well aware that she danced only for him.

The first two scenes of the ballet went smoothly and Carrie geared herself up for the third and final scene, the carnival scene when she realises that Casimir, in a fit of blind fury at her adultery, has killed their child. She drank a bit of water as she stood in the wings and practised a few pliés at the moveable barre to loosen her back and legs. The music of the orchestra was fast and furious and she could hear the pounding of feet on the boards as the corps danced. She could see the costumes of the girls swirling in and out of view; crimson, green, royal blue, glittering with sequins and gold braid.

A touch on her shoulder made her turn. 'Ready?' asked Casimir. Like her, he was dressed in sombre black, his broad shoulders straining against the shoulders of his short jacket, his legs long and muscular in their dark tights.

'Break a leg?' she hazarded.

He tugged on the long swathe of her hair which now hung loose down her back. 'Go out there and kill 'em, cat,' he said.

'Tiger,' Carrie corrected him. 'Kill 'em, tiger.' He was just beginning to walk away when she added in a casual tone, 'Bonnie made a confession today.'

Casimir turned, a sudden tension in his muscles. 'A confession about what?'

'You.' Carrie gave him a conspiratorial smile. 'She said she's madly in love with you.'

Casimir's grin split his face, turning his blue eyes into half-moons. '*Lapushka!*' he exclaimed, reaching for her and about to lift her exultantly in his arms, when a stagehand came up to them.

'Miss Moore? Your cue,' he said, and Carrie stiffened, waiting for the roll of the drum that would bring her out on stage in this, the most exhausting scene she would ever dance.

The first step out of the wings brought her against the backdrop where she stood hesitantly, in an attitude of fear and flight, sylphlike, all in black from the long sleeves of her leotard to the tips of her black pointe shoes, only her pale face, hands and the long swathe of honey-brown hair relieving the dark effect.

She began to run through the dancers, weaving in and out of their patterns, now bumping into one or being grabbed by another. She sought Casimir, her husband, the murderer of her child; she felt the hatred swell up in her, ballooning in her chest until she thought she would burst. In the wings, Casimir shook his arms in preparation for their pas de deux, for the moment when he would enter on the stage and Carrie would throw herself at him. He would have to lift her high above the other dancers, the muscles in his arms bulging as he began to leap.

Carrie danced the pas de deux as she had in rehearsal, summoning every bit of lyricism and technique that she possessed. The grief was there; the anger was there; but the ferocity of her emotions was tempered by something else, and it was this that caused the critics to later rave over 'Caroline Moore's emotional depth and intensity in *Revenge Motif*.'

On this night, Carrie felt pity for Casimir, for the grief that he must be suffering, and the incandescent edge of her dancing was softened by this unexpected empathy. Casimir felt it and responded, and the dance, harsh and angry, was underlined by their mutual mourning for the betrayal of their love and for the death of their child. At its end, when Casimir forcibly held her in his embrace,

Carrie didn't fight him the way she had in rehearsal; she clung to him, her face against the damp fabric of his leotard, feeling his heart racing beneath her cheek, his chest rising and falling in a rapid tempo. She too was sweating, her hair tangled around her face, her legs trembling with fatigue. With the child gone, with Stephan gone, she had nothing else but this man who had been her husband, her lover and the father of her child. Who else could share the savage intensity of her loss?

They stood in that embrace as the curtain descended, the applause from the audience thundering through its heavy velvet folds. Gregory was making victory signs in the wings and Veronica was shaking her head in admiration. Casimir patted Carrie on the back as they separated, and then they stood together holding hands as the curtain rose once more, to reveal an audience on its feet, shouting and screaming. Flowers began to hit the stage, and Carrie picked up a rose and then curtsied, causing the audience to roar even louder. She trembled slightly, the fear that always followed a triumph haunting her at even this moment. She could never completely savour a success; failure always lurked around the corner, waiting for her at the next performance.

Casimir pulled her to her feet. 'Congratulations,' he whispered, and she threw her arms around, him, kissing him on the mouth and then pushing him forward for his own bow and acclaim. Casimir had danced superlatively, and Carrie knew that without him her ballet would have been nothing.

After the curtain calls, the backstage area hummed with excited dancers. Carrie personally made the rounds, thanking some and complimenting others. Each and every one, she knew, had contributed to the success of *Revenge Motif*, and for some, it had been their debut with the company. Exhausted but full of a quiet elation, she slipped away into her dressing room where she washed off her stage make-up, showered and slipped into the dress that Bonnie had brought for her. Since the dancers would all be present at the party, no one had been allowed to visit the dressing rooms. Only Veronica came to congratulate her, and they smiled at one another, both knowing how important the older dancer's contribution had been to Carrie's new interpretation of the last scene.

Carrie arrived at the party to find it was going full blast, the reception room of the hotel filled with elegantly clad guests holding glasses of champagne. The room had been decorated with ballet motifs. Full-length posters advertising *Revenge Motif* were hung on its walls, and Carrie found herself staring at her own image with Casimir, his hand on her waist as she stood poised in an arabesque. Ballet shoes hung from the chandeliers, and Carrie could see an ice sculpture of a ballerina standing in a large silver bowl in the centre of a long table of hors d'oeuvres.

She stood in an archway, watching the glittering crowd, her hair braided into a coronet on her head, her body slender and curvaceous in a long teal-blue silk gown that left one shoulder bare, her feet in silver high-heeled sandals. For a second, she was left on her own, then someone recognised her and she was besieged by admirers. She smiled and nodded, slowly working her way through the throng, looking for her parents, praying that they had arrived in time to see the ballet and hoping that she would be able to spot them in the crush. Instead, she came face to face with Leona Sole, tall and glamorous in aquamarine chiffon, a frosted glass in one hand.

'Miss Moore,' she said. 'You were brilliant as always.'

'Thank you.' Carrie tried to be polite, but her eyes kept wandering past Leona's bare white shoulders.

'Alex and I were lucky to get a box,' the other woman continued.

Alex's name caught Carrie's attention. 'He's with

you?' she asked with a frown. For some reason, she had been under the impression that Alex and Bonnie had come togethr to the gala.

'He's always with me when I'm in New York,' Leona explained.

Carrie looked into her slanted green eyes, their expression haughty and imperious. 'Is he?' she asked as all her anticipation and joy began to drain away.

'Yes, aren't you, darling?' Leona beckoned to the tall man in a dark suit who was coming through the crowd to stand at her side.

'Aren't I what?' Alex asked.

'With me when I'm in New York.'

Alex didn't answer her but looked down at Carrie, his dark eyes full of anger. 'You danced superbly,' he said, his voice cold and derisive.

Carrie stared at him, shock making her breath come short. What had she done to deserve . . . ?

'And your partner was wonderful as well,' Leona inserted, twining her arm through Alex's. 'Can we anticipate an engagement, Miss Moore?'

'An engagement?' Carrie asked in bewilderment.

'That kiss, Miss Moore,' said Leona with a trace of mockery in her voice. 'It was quite a performance of its own.'

Carrie threw Alex a wild glance. 'It was nothing more than a way of . . . saying thank you,' she stammered. Didn't Alex understand? Surely he didn't imagine that her kiss for Casimir had held anything more than affection?

Leona's laughter tinkled like shards of falling glass. 'I'll have to be as enthusiastic when I say thank you.' She glanced up at the man at her side, her eyes flickering uneasily from the hard line of his mouth to Carrie's sudden pallor. 'Don't you agree, darling?'

Carrie stiffened herself for his response, knowing that it would hurt when it came, but she was saved by

Gregory's intervention. 'Carrie! There you are; I've been looking all over for you. There's a dozen people that I want you to meet.' He gave Leona and Alex a perfunctory smile as he grabbed Carrie's hand. 'I hope you don't mind if I take her away for a few minutes?'

'Not at all,' said Alex, his expression indifferent. 'She's all yours.' And he turned on his heel, his arm around Leona, as if talking to Carrie were the last thing on earth he wanted to do.

Gregory bounced as he was apt to do when the Manhattan Ballet Company was successful. 'Now, let me introduce you to . . .'

Carrie allowed herself to be led away, all her hope and happy anticipation sagging under the weight of a new burden. She followed Gregory around, greeting various patrons of the ballet. It was standard procedure for an opening night, and Carrie smiled and nodded and talked as if she had nothing more on her mind than the evening's success.

'You were stunning, Miss Moore!'

'A real star.'

'It was a thrill to watch you . . .'

'Are you planning another ballet?'

Carrie fielded all the compliments and the questions like a pro, taking the proper line between modesty and pride, and all the while she longed to run into a corner and hide. How, she wondered miserably, could she have been so foolish and naïve as to believe what Bonnie had told her? Alex didn't love her; he disliked her intensely, and she realised with despair that it hadn't been Bonnie's arms that she had driven him to, but Leona's. When she thought about some of the things that she had said to him, Carrie could blame no one but herself. The evening she had met him in the nightclub, she had told him, in no uncertain terms, that she never wanted to have a husband or child. Why now should she think that Alex understood the message she had sent him through her dancing? There was no unity of spirit between them; there was nothing at all left except the hurtful edge of his hostility and her own misery.

Her glow of warm expectation had died away completely, and she now understood how blind she had been. She had been so carried away by Bonnie's words and the promise in them that she had thought that Alex must feel the same way. She had assumed, quite erroneously, that he had been sitting around, twiddling his thumbs so to speak, waiting for her to come to the realisation that they were mutually in love. She couldn't have been more naïve, Carrie thought to herself as she escaped from Gregory at last and made her way into a quiet corridor. Alex had found solace elsewhere and, in the process, had transferred whatever love he had felt for her to someone else. Veronica had warned her that she might lose him for ever, and her words had obviously been prophetic. Carrie knew when she was beaten; she knew . . .

She turned down another hallway, then stopped abruptly. A couple stood entwined before her, their mouths meeting in a passionate kiss, their fair heads almost the same shade of gold under the light. Carrie hastily turned away so she wouldn't interrupt them. It was Bonnie and Casimir, and it wasn't hard to guess what must have transpired between them. In the midst of her own misery, she was happy for them and offered a silent prayer for their future, hoping that two such dominating, flirtatious personalities could live within the confines of a relationship without destroying one another. She didn't think it would be easy, but what Casimir and Bonnie lacked in harmony, they more than made up for in passion. Only time would tell if it would suffice.

'Carrie! We've been looking all over for you!' Elizabeth and Joshua Moore were walking towards her, proud smiles on their faces.

'Mom!' Carrie exclaimed, rushing into her mother's

arms and then her father's. 'Where have you been? Did you get to see the ballet?'

Elizabeth tucked her arm through Carrie's. 'Honey, you were wonderful, and the ballet was terrific!'

Joshua patted her hand. 'We lost the address of the hotel or we would have been here sooner.'

'Not we, Josh—you lost the address. Honestly, Carrie, I thought I'd kill him! We ended up taking a tour of downtown Manhattan.'

Carrie gave them both a smile. 'Just as long as you made it,' she said. She was surprised to discover just how nice it was to see them. Her mother looked elegant in a long grey gown, pearls at her throat; her father tall and distinguished in his tuxedo. They represented all the good things in Carrie's life; comfort, security and love, and just having them at her side gave her a feeling of protection.

'Want to meet the crowd?' she asked.

'Of course,' said her father. 'Lead on.'

Her parents had met some of the dancers when the company had been in San Francisco, but not all of them, and Carrie introduced them to everyone. When they had finally had a drink of champagne and were beginning to look weary after their long day of plane journeys, performance and conversation, Carrie suggested that they leave.

'You're staying at the apartment, aren't you?' she asked.

'Nope,' said Elizabeth, taking Joshua's hand and smiling up at him. 'We're booked into a hotel.'

'But there's no need . . .'

'Call it a second honeymoon, honey,' said her father.

'Oh,' she said, and grinned. 'You're both a pair of romantics!'

'That's us,' Elizabeth agreed, then she caught sight of someone beyond Carrie, her face beaming with delight. 'Alex! How good to see you!'

'Elizabeth,' he said, leaning over and kissing Carrie's mother on the cheek. 'Joshua.' He shook the older man's hand, and they began to talk about travelling and future plans while Carrie stared at them, remembering Julie's statement that Alex often visited her parents when he was in San Francisco.

'Are you here alone?' her mother asked, and Alex explained that he had brought a date, but she was flying back to San Francisco tonight with her father and that, in fact, she was already gone.

Elizabeth threw Carrie an odd look as Joshua asked, 'Will we have a chance to see you before we leave New York?'

'I'd like to,' Alex responded. He didn't even glance at Carrie; she might as well have been invisible for all he was concerned, and she glared furiously at his handsome profile and the indentation which appeared in his lean cheek as he smiled at her father. 'Let me jot down my address and phone number for you.'

They made arrangements while Carrie fumed, her toe tapping the floor beneath the hem of her long dress. What right, she thought furiously, had Alex to forge such an affectionate connection with her family? They had nothing in common; there was no reason that they had to be such friends. All the misery that Alex had made her feel now turned itself into a blazing white fury which only increased as Alex said goodbye, giving her only the slightest of nods as he left, his dark eyes cold and mocking. Carrie didn't even deign to give him the benefit of her attention. She looked away as he left, staring at the now melting ice ballerina that adorned the depleted table of hors d'oeuvres. Her arabesque was sagging, her stretched-out leg had melted away, her hands were gone. There were only a few people left in the room, and Carrie's fury suddenly dissipated, leaving her feeling weary, unhappy and depressed. She sighed deeply, missing her parents' concerned looks and the conspiratorial glance between them. Her father excused himself for a minute, and Elizabeth suggested that they wait for him on a bench in the corridor.

'Carrie,' she asked with a worried frown as they sat down, 'what's happened between you and Alex?'

Carrie shrugged. 'Nothing,' she said, barely noticing the look that passed between her parents and her father's nod as he walked away.

'We know about the baby,' Elizabeth said softly.

Carrie looked in shock at her mother's round face framed in curly brown hair. 'Julie told you?' she whispered.

'No, darling, Alex did.'

'Oh, God!' Carrie exclaimed, her voice a groan of agony as she covered her face with her hands.

Elizabeth stroked Carrie's back. 'It's all right, honey. Daddy and I don't mind.'

Carrie dropped her hands and stared at them. 'It was all a mistake. I was so stupid.'

'Everyone makes mistakes,' Elizabeth said soothingly. 'I only wish you had told us, and I'm sorry that I wasn't with you when you lost the baby. I know just how hard it is.'

'Do you?' Carrie whispered. Could anyone with two healthy daughters understand what it was like to lose the only one she had?

Elizabeth seemed to recognise the direction of Carrie's thoughts. 'I was pregnant before I had Julie, and I miscarried. It would have been our son.'

Carrie looked at her mother in surprise. 'You never told us.'

Elizabeth gave her a wavering smile. 'It wasn't an ordinary subject of conversation, and it made me cry to talk about it.' She took Carrie's hand and squeezed it. 'No woman ever forgets the children she's carried. One just has to believe that nature intended these things to happen.'

'It was my fault,' said Carrie. 'The baby was healthy.'

'The pregnancy wasn't healthy,' Elizabeth countered firmly. 'Think about it that way.'

Carrie took a deep breath. 'I'm sorry I didn't tell you. I should have trusted you more.'

Her mother patted her hand. 'We love you, honey, and we want you to be happy. That's why we're so concerned about Alex.'

'You don't have to be concerned. We had a short-lived affair and it's been over ever since.'

'From whose perspective?'

'Mine and his. He dislikes me; you saw the way he treated me just now.'

'Carrie, you've put him through hell,' Elizabeth said and, although her voice was gentle, her brown eyes were stern.

'I should have told him about the baby, I suppose.' Carrie spread her hands apart in a helpless gesture. 'But it wouldn't have made any difference. He doesn't love me.'

Elizabeth looked at her in surprise. 'Do you love him?'

Carrie's mouth turned down. 'Yes, for all it's worth.'

'He loves you, honey,' Elizabeth said intently. 'It would seem that everyone in the family knows it except you. And he loved that baby.'

Carrie gave her a look of disbelief. 'Mom, you must be seeing Alex through rose-coloured glasses! He was worried about the baby's paternity, not about her health. It was a matter of pride, not fatherhood.'

Elizabeth sat up straight, her face shocked. 'How can you be so heartless?' she asked.

'Heartless?' Carrie asked in stunned incredulity.

'If ever a man wanted a child, it was Alex. Carrie, he cried when he told us that you'd lost the baby. He sat in our living room and he cried.'

CHAPTER TEN

LATER, Carrie was never quite sure how her parents
managed to convince her that she should go to Alex's
apartment, but all she knew was that she found herself in
her coat and in a taxi going uptown with the note Alex
had jotted down for her father clutched in her hand. It
was close to midnight and, although she had protested
that it was far too late for her to be visiting, her parents
had insisted, their faces and voices adamant. As the
lights of Broadway vanished behind the taxi, Carrie
thought briefly of telling the driver to turn around and
head back to her apartment, but then she decided that
Casimir and Bonnie would be there and she knew that
she had no intention of interrupting that amorous idyll.

It would seem, she reflected wryly, that she had
nowhere to go except into the lion's den. She stared out
the taxi's window at the traffic around them and wondered idly where all the other New Yorkers were hurry-
ing at this hour. She had lived in Manhattan for so long
that she had lost her initial awe and disbelief at the vast
numbers of people who kept the city moving all day and
night. New York throbbed with life at times when other
cities had rolled up their sidewalks and shut down for
slumber as if it were a huge animal, never sleeping and
constantly on the prowl. Carrie had never thought about
her adjustment from suburban to urban life, but she now
realised how very much she loved Manhattan's frenetic
pace. She missed it when she went away; her artistic life
thrived on its excitement.

The screech of another taxi and the blaring of horns
roused Carrie from her thoughts and she peered at the
buildings they were passing. Alex lived at an exclusive

address at Central Park West, and they were drawing near it, passing a line of horse-drawn carriages that carried families of tourists through the city by day and lovers at night. Business appeared to be slow; the horses were asleep, their blinkered heads hanging down, and the drivers were leaning against their coaches, rubbing their hands together in the cool night air. Carrie's taxi passed swiftly by, jockeyed around a small traffic jam at one corner and then swept up before an imposing building with a canopied front and a doorman.

She took a deep breath, paid the driver, then stepped out on to the sidewalk, barely noticing the clarity of the stars overhead or the brilliance of the April moon. She was now wondering whether Alex would even let her get beyond the doorman. It hadn't occurred to her before that he might turn her away, but it did now. She hesitated, trying to think up one good reason why he should welcome her. Nothing came to mind, and Carrie ironically reflected as she entered the building that it might be quite possible that she would have nowhere to go tonight except a hotel.

The doorman gave her an appreciative look, called Alex's apartment and then said she could go on up. Carrie breathed a sigh that mixed relief and apprehension in its exhalation and took the elevator to the penthouse suite, nervously smoothing the long lines of her dress, her heart beginning to pound in fear.

The penthouse had a double set of wooden doors with brass handles, and Carrie hesitated before raising her hand to the panel, trying hard to remember her parents' persuasive arguments about why she should be there. Everyone had insisted that Alex loved her, but she wouldn't believe it until she heard it herself, and she strongly suspected that hell would freeze over before Alex would speak of love to her. Actions spoke louder than words, and Alex had not shown her anything but the hard face of his dislike. No, it wasn't his supposed love for her that had persuaded Carrie to come tonight, but the poignant image of Alex crying in front of her parents. The loss of their child had brought him to tears, and Carrie desperately wanted to apologise for her denial of his grief. As her mother had said, she had been heartless, and the least she could do was beg Alex's forgiveness for her unwarranted and devastating cruelty.

She knocked at last and the double doors opened. Alex stood there, his jacket and tie missing, his white shirt unbuttoned to reveal the tanned column of his throat and the deep hollow carved by his shoulder blades. Carrie remembered placing her lips there and she trembled, clutching her evening bag before her breasts.

Alex eyed her with indifference. His black hair was rumpled as if he had run his fingers roughly through the strands and he held a half-finished glass of whisky in his lean hands. 'What do you want?' he asked.

Carrie took a deep breath. 'Can I come in?'

'If you want to,' he replied carelessly.

She followed him into a large living room which was carpeted in white and decorated in brown and black leather. There was a large, teak unit which held many books and glassware, original oil paintings on two walls and soft music coming from a hidden stereo. One entire wall was made of window, and Carrie exclaimed at the panoramic vista of the New York skyline whose lights glittered and sparkled like jewels tossed carelessly against the backdrop of a black velvet sky.

'What a wonderful view!'

'I like it,' he said coldly. 'Do you want a drink?'

Carrie shook her head as she took her coat off and placed it on the couch. 'No, thank you.' She sat down and looked at him. He was standing by the window, the harsh lines of his face barely softened by the yellow gleam of a nearby lamp. The fear Carrie had felt on entering his apartment now altered to an aching in her heart. She wondered which of those lines had been etched by the death of their daughter, and she longed to go to him and gently trace those markings of grief and mourning as if her fingers could soothe them away.

'Well,' he said, 'are you here for a reason?'

'I . . . feel that I owe you an apology.'

'About what?' he said curtly.

'About the baby,' said Carrie, clearing her throat, unhappily aware that while she wanted to offer Alex her apologies and sympathy, the act of doing so was going to be difficult indeed.

'There's nothing to say,' he grated. 'She's dead.'

Carrie winced but forged ahead. 'I'm sorry that I said such cruel things to you. I had no idea how you really felt. I couldn't understand that . . . that you felt as strongly about the baby as I did.'

Alex's mouth slanted wryly and he took a sip of his drink. 'How generous of you!'

Carrie supposed she deserved the treatment Alex was giving her, but that didn't make his cynicism any easier to bear. Didn't he understand that she was offering him a means of making peace and a way of sharing their loss?

'I mean it,' she said angrily.

Alex shrugged his broad shoulders. 'I'm sure you do, but don't you think it's a little late to be offering apologies? It happened seven months ago, not yesterday.'

'You're making this so hard for me,' Carrie said helplessly.

Alex put his glass down on a nearby table with such force that some of the liquor spilled over its edge. 'Why should I make it easy for you?' he grated. 'Did you have any thought for what I went through, first finding out that I was going to be a father and then that I had no child at all in the same evening? Because that's how it happened. I talked to Casimir at a party, realised that you'd lied to me and then had Bonnie tell me that you'd lost her.'

'I know I should have told . . .'

He jammed his hands into the pockets of his slacks. 'Why didn't you? I've never understood that.'

'I was afraid that you'd insist on marrying me.'

'Of course,' he said sarcastically, 'I should have known. You're the one who can't bear any sort of relationship because it might interfere with your dancing. Maybe that's the way it should be. The only time I've ever seen you alive is when you're on stage.'

Carrie flinched. 'I have very warm friendships,' she said defensively.

'Friendships!' Alex snorted in disgust. 'I'm talking about relating to a man.'

'I don't have trouble with men,' she retorted.

'Oh, yes,' he said mockingly, 'I've forgotten Casimir.'

'Casimir and I were never lovers.'

'No? You mean you couldn't handle sex with Casimir either?'

Carrie was so angry she shook. 'What are you insinuating?'

'That you're afraid of any man who sees you as more than a celebrity or a stage personality, as a flesh-and-blood woman with human needs and sexual drives. To go to bed with me you had to pretend you were someone else.'

'You were the first man . . .' she whispered.

Alex picked up his drink and took a long swallow. 'And you proved that it was no particular honour,' he said harshly.

Carrie glanced away from the derision in his eyes to the panorama behind him, but she wasn't seeing that splendid vista at all. She was wondering if Alex wasn't right. Had she had spent most of her life hiding behind her identity as a dancer? She had always been shy; she hadn't been able to talk easily to other people except for her immediate family and her fellow dancers. Was that why she had been so devoted to her career? Because she saw it as camouflage, as protection, against the outside world? She had always thought of dancing as her destiny and that her talent was a gift she must enjoy to the hilt, but now she saw that her dedication had arisen from fear as well as from ability, warping her view of life and narrowing it until she could see and feel nothing beyond the perimeters of the ballet world.

She looked slowly back at Alex, who was now gazing out of the window, his profile dark against the sky, and understood that no one could help her but herself. She had to break the mould that confined her and fight her own reluctance to reveal her vulnerabilities. When she was on stage, she could wear her heart on her sleeve, knowing that she was shielded by the artifice of ballet, but now she had no such protection. She was stripped of her anger and her defences; she had nothing else but her love, and that held no value for anyone except the tall man before her whose rigid posture suggested that if she laid it before him, he would grind it beneath the hell of his disgust.

Carrie clenched her hands into small fists as she contemplated revealing herself and confessing the ultimate weakness. If Alex laughed in her face, would she be able to leave with any semblance of dignity? She teetered on the edge of indecision; afraid and yet desperate. If she walked away now, Carrie knew there would be no returning, no second chance to heal the breach between them. Alex would be lost to her for ever, and she didn't know whether she could bear another loss and another cause for grief. Yet she was terrified of offering to him the most fragile and delicate of her emotions. She would be broken, Carrie knew, broken and shattered by even the slightest hint of indifference or derision.

She stood up and Alex turned towards her. 'Are

you leaving?' he asked with only a modicum of politeness.

God, this was going to be hard! 'No.'

One dark eyebrow arched in mockery. 'You have more sins to confess.'

'Not exactly a sin.'

'A confession, then? How interesting!'

Carrie felt her knees beginning to tremble and knew that if she put off the words any longer, she would lose her determination. 'I . . . love you,' she said, her voice high, breathless and shaky.

The words hung between them as Alex stared at her, his face unreadable. She felt a bubble of hysterical laughter rising within her. She had expected anything from sarcasm to acceptance, but not this silence, this long examination of her face and then an almost clinical study of her body in its long blue dress.

When he spoke his voice cut the silence like a knife. 'What did you say?'

Carrie now trembled in earnest. 'I said that I love you.'

The line of his mouth turned cold, cruel and contemptuous. 'Prove it,' he said.

Carrie swallowed, swaying slightly on her silver heels. The carpet was so deep that she made no sound as she walked over to him and only the soft swishing of her silk dress against her legs could be heard in the room. Their eyes locked and Carrie clung to that visual bond as if it were the only support that kept her from collapsing on her shaking legs. When she reached him, she sought desperately for some softening in his dark eyes, some indication that he would welcome what she was about to do. But nothing had changed. Alex was still, waiting and tense, one hand jammed in a pocket, the other holding on to his glass.

Carrie was vibrantly aware of the man before her. There was a small nick on his chin from shaving and his beard was starting to grow again, its shadow dark against his skin. She could see the way his shirt stretched tautly over his chest and, in the V of its unbuttoned collar, dark hairs curled against his planes of his muscles. His abdomen was flat and athletic, his hips narrow, his legs long and lean in their well-cut slacks. She moved up against him until her silk-tipped breasts brushed against his chest, then stood on tiptoe, placing her tremulous mouth against his, tantalising his lips with hers.

For several minutes, she tried to arouse him with her mouth, but Alex didn't respond and Carrie moved backwards, her eyes hurt and bewildered. He gazed mockingly down into their golden depths. 'You give up easily, don't you?' she asked.

He was so cold and seemingly uninterested that Carrie felt helpless, but one small spark of hope remained within her; he hadn't rebuffed her, he hadn't pushed her away. She took a deep breath and reached out to unbutton his shirt, her fingers slow and hesitant. When she reached his waistline, she stopped, touching the soft hairs that curled around his navel, and Alex's sudden indrawn breath told her all that she needed to know. Now she smiled slightly as she slid her hands up his bared chest, feeling his muscles rippling under her palms, his skin warm and smooth. She widened the opening of his shirt, pulling it back across his shoulders so that his torso was bare, and leaned forward so she could trace a line across his chest with her mouth and tongue.

Suddenly his glass was put down abruptly and his arm went around her like a steel band, bringing her up to him. 'Carrie,' he groaned, and his mouth came down on hers, their lips meeting with an urgency that came of utter need and desire.

Their clothes were a hindrance, barriers to their passion, and Carrie's dress fell into a soft blue pool of shimmering silk at her feet, her lacy underthings beside it. Alex undressed with one arm around her so that her bared breasts touched his chest, and she could feel the heavy pounding of his heart against her flesh. His arousal was hot against the curve of her thighs and insistent, and she caressed him as they sank to the carpeted floor, the lamplight turning their skin golden and shadowed in its soft beam.

They made love wildly and without speaking, no word was uttered since he had spoken her name. It was as if language was not sufficient; they needed the blazing contact of physical unity to burn away the cold months of their separation. They touched at mouth, breast, hip and toe, every inch of their bodies craving and hungering for contact. Alex's hands were in possession of her body; his touch knowing, his mouth seductive. His hand raised the swell of her breast to his mouth; his fingers traced a path down her abdomen that was later followed by his tongue. Carrie moaned as he kissed her intimately, a molten flood of passion turning her weak and languorous. When he finally opened her legs and entered her, she was mindless, lost in a world of unbelievable sensation, the spiralling rise of her desire breaking until she felt as if she were falling into a void; dark, warm and velvet.

When it was over, Alex lay on top of her, his breath still harsh and ragged from passion. Carrie idly ran her hand down the curve of his spine, feeling the dampness of his skin, exulting in the hardness of bone and muscle beneath her fingertips. She felt triumphant and assured, so different from the woman who had entered the flat an hour earlier. She had learned the power of her body during their lovemaking and the strength of Alex's feeling for her. He had wanted her with every fibre of his being; he had trembled beneath her caress. She no longer doubted what her friends and family had told her; she only wished she had realised it earlier. Hours and days had been wasted, lost to unwarranted misery and unhappiness.

Alex rolled off her and propped himself up on one

elbow, looking down into her face, the amber eyes softened to gold, her skin flushed from lovemaking. 'You could get pregnant again,' he said.

'Mmmm.' She placed her mouth on his bare shoulder and licked it.

'You don't seem alarmed.' There was a smile in his dark eyes.

'I'm not.'

'I thought you didn't want a husband or children.'

Carrie gave him a mischievous grin. 'You mean I can have both?'

Alex ran a finger along the edge of her cheek. 'Do you want them?'

'Is this a proposal?' she queried, her voice teasing.

He looked at her, his face serious. 'Your career has always come between us.'

'It's my fault,' Carrie said. 'I was the one who made it an obstacle. It doesn't have to be.'

'Even in Florida, it was there.'

'I was so afraid that a man would want me because I was Caroline Moore, ballerina—and yet,' she paused thoughtfully, 'you were right. I also hid behind my dancer façade. I've always been afraid to let my emotions out; it seemed safer to bury them in my dancing.'

Alex turned her face towards his, his hand cupping her chin. 'Carrie, you mustn't hide from me. I don't want a dancer, I want a wife. I want a woman with strong desires and powerful emotions. I want to know what you're thinking and feeling.'

Carrie gave him a tremulous smile. 'I'm feeling very nice right now!'

'If I'd known that all it took was lying naked on my living room carpet,' Alex growled, 'I would have dragged you up here months ago.'

Carrie wrapped her arms around his muscular waist and hugged him tight. 'I'm so sorry for all the time we lost.'

'So am I.' Alex buried his face in her hair. He had pulled it down from its coronet during their lovemaking, the hairpins falling and scattering around them. Her braids had loosened and long strands of her hair lay like wisps of honey-brown smoke in the carpet around her head.

'Alex?'

'Mmmm?'

'Are you and Leona lovers?' It took Carrie courage to ask that, because if the answer was wrong, she knew it would hurt.

'*Were* lovers,' Alex said, correcting her. 'Several years ago. We've been friends since, although she would like to get something going again.'

'Oh.'

He pinched the plumpest portion of her anatomy. 'You're smiling,' he said.

'Ouch! Well, I was jealous.'

'Were you?' he asked in astonishment. 'Then why didn't my dating Bonnie make you jealous?'

'It did,' she confessed. 'I was miserable, but I couldn't do anything. I didn't want to interfere. She's my best friend.'

Alex gave a groan. 'We thought it wasn't working. She told me she'd never known you to get upset over a man.' He lay back on the floor and stared at the ceiling. 'God, what a waste!'

'Did you begin dating her just to find me?'

'I couldn't believe my luck when I met her at the party. Do you have any idea how crazy I went trying to find you?'

Carrie leaned on her elbow and traced a line down the centre of his chest where the V of dark hair angled towards his abdomen. 'You mean after Naples?'

'I called every Hughes in the Manhattan phone book, and when that didn't work I tried all the advertising firms. I couldn't believe that you'd lied to me like that.'

'I thought you were so angry with me that you wouldn't care.'

'I wasn't angry, I was furious. I wanted to kill you that day on the beach! I was determined to forget that you existed, but I couldn't get you out of my mind.'

'I'm glad,' she said, her finger moving lower than his abdomen until he grabbed her wrist and growled, 'If you don't stop that, I won't answer for the consequences!'

'Maybe I like the consequences,' she said sweetly.

Alex suddenly tumbled her over on her back and pressed her shoulders to the floor with his hands. 'You have some explaining to do first,' he said. 'Are you and Casimir lovers?'

Carrie looked up into his face and saw the tension there. 'I told you we weren't.'

His voice was curt. 'Say it again.'

'I went out with him because you were dating Bonnie. He never really wanted me, you know. He's crazy about Bonnie, and vice versa. I caught them in a passionate embrace in the hotel.'

'What about that kiss on stage? The press is going to go berserk over it.'

Carrie grimaced. 'I know,' she said. 'It was an impulsive gesture; he danced magnificently.'

'So did you.'

'Did you understand the third scene?' Carrie asked shyly.

Alex reached up and smoothed a tendril of hair on her temple. 'I knew that you were expressing a sadness and empathy with Casimir and that the death of the child united you in grief.'

'I was dancing for you,' she said. 'I wanted you to know how I felt.'

Alex brushed his lips softly against hers. 'I wondered if the ballet was about us, but I couldn't bear thinking about it. I was so angry at you and so frustrated. There were times when I hated you.'

Carrie wound her arms around her neck and pulled him down for a far more thorough kiss. 'Does that make it better?' she asked.

'You know it does,' he said softly. 'I love you. I always have, from the moment I saw you in the moonlight in Naples. You were like some sort of a dream; a goddess on a starlit night with the smell of sea air in her hair and the body of an angel. I hadn't believed in love at first sight and I've never felt that way about a woman before, but when we made love that night I knew we were meant for one another.'

'I fell in love with you then, too,' Carrie gave a low laugh, 'but I preferred to believe it was just an infatuation. Too much moon and Piña Coladas!'

'You were a little tipsy,' Alex teased.

'Tipsy and foolish.'

There was a short pause. 'Foolish and pregnant,' he said slowly. 'You must have been shocked when you found out about the baby.'

'I wanted to die,' Carrie told him, recalling that moment with a reminiscent shiver.

'Are you cold?' he asked, pulling her into his arms.

'No.'

'We could go into the bedroom,' he said. 'There's a wonderful queen-size bed in there with pillows and blankets.'

Carrie didn't dare break the momentum of the evening. 'I find I'm becoming very fond of your living room carpet,' she said. 'I can look up and see the stars and low-flying airplanes.' She pointed towards the wall of window before them. The star-studded black sky arched over them; the moon hung like an ivory disc on a stage backdrop. It was peaceful where they were. The room was warm, the carpet thick and the lamplight dim. Carrie suddenly noticed that the stereo was still playing, an orchestrated popular song muted and soft.

Alex stretched and reached up to the couch, pulling

down a large cushion and a brown and gold afghan. He tucked the cushion under their head and spread the quilt over them. 'Just in case,' he said, pulling her back into the warm curve of his shoulder. 'I don't want you to get sick.'

'It's nice,' she said, fingering its scalloped edge. 'Did someone make it?'

'My mother,' he said wryly. 'She showers me with hand-knitted socks and sweaters, afghans and quilts.'

'Do you think your parents will like me?' Carrie asked hesitantly.

'They'll love you; they're dying for me to settle down. The whole family has been matchmaking for years. Andrew says he's tired of carrying the burden of having the only grandchildren. Besides, they all know about you.'

Carrie struggled in his arms. 'Alex! You didn't tell them . . .'

'No,' he said, holding her firmly against him, 'I didn't tell them about the baby, only that I'd met the woman I wanted to marry.'

'I wondered when you were finally going to get to the proposal,' she said archly.

Alex laughed. 'Haven't I asked you yet?'

'Not formally.'

'And I don't suppose you're the kind of woman who can do without the formalities.'

'If you don't mind, I want to hear the first and last marriage proposal I'm ever going to get.' Carrie returned his pinch. 'Come on, Mr Taylor, get on with it!'

There was a short silence and then Alex spoke, his voice suddenly serious and sombre. 'Carrie, will you marry me and give me more children? I'm thirty-four and I want another daughter.'

A sob caught in Carrie's throat. 'Oh, Alex,' she sighed, 'I wished she was alive. I think about her every day.'

His arm tightened around her. 'When I found out that you'd had a girl, I had a vision in my mind of a little girl that looked like you with big golden eyes and a head of brown curls. I could imagine having her here, decorating a room for her, taking her to the zoo.' His voice broke slightly and Carrie closed her eyes, her hands clutching his. 'I'd never thought much about fatherhood before. It seemed like something that would happen to me far off in the future, but when I suddenly learned how close it had come, I found out that I wanted it very much. I was devastated when I went to see you in the Rockaways. I . . . wanted you to know how I felt, how empty I was.'

Carrie pulled herself upwards so she could bury her face in Alex's neck. How lonely they had both been, fighting their grief in isolation. If only she had reached out to him then; if only she had been able to show her emotions instead of burying them deep and hoping they would disappear. Instead, they had waged a constant conflict within her, causing her sleepless nights and an estrangement from Alex that had been both futile and unhappy.

Her tears dampened his skin and Alex moved sideways so he could see her face. 'Darling,' he said gently, 'don't cry.'

Carrie gave a shaky sigh. 'I was so angry with you, Alex, that I only saw you as an enemy. It wasn't until much later that Veronica made me see that my fury came from a feeling of being abandoned. I know I kept pushing you away, but underneath I needed you so badly. I wanted you in the hospital with me.'

'Next time,' said Alex, pressing his lips gently to the corner of her eye where a tear seeped out from under an eyelid. 'Next time I'll be with you. I love you, Carrie. I promise I won't leave your side.'

The babies tumbled on the carpet, their fat little hands grabbing for the colourful plastic toys. They had black

curls and eyes that had gone from a royal blue to a
strange shade of brown that Elizabeth swore would turn
to amber in a few weeks. Otherwise, they looked just
like pictures of Alex and Andrew when they were
babies. One was more solemn than the other; he tended
to suck his thumb. The other grinned and preferred his
toes. Carrie and Alex liked to lay a big blanket on the
carpet in the living room and put the babies there after
dinner. Alex would lie on the floor and play with them,
letting them tug on his hair and nose or throwing them
into the air, while Carrie threatened him with death if he
upset their stomachs.

'You're a glutton for punishment,' she threatened
when he winced as Mark yanked on his ear.

'I know; I'm stuck for life,' he said, grinning at her.

'It was your choice,' she reminded him severely,
eyeing him over her knitting needles.

Alex pulled himself up on the couch and put his arm
around her. 'Happy?' he asked.

'Ferociously,' she said with a smile.

'You don't mind missing the ballet season?'

'Seasons,' she reminded him.

'Sometimes when your feet twitch at night, I think you
must be dreaming about dancing again.'

'I do miss it,' she said, 'but I've also liked being a
choreographer, and besides, I'm going back in a few
months. Veronica says she's looking forward to getting
me back in shape after another pregnancy. She enjoys
being a slave-driver!'

Alex nibbled at her earlobe. 'I like the shape you're
in,' he murmured, and Carrie blushed. She had put on
weight during her pregnancy and her slender figure was
more voluptuous and curved than it had ever been.

'None of that,' she said, giving his roving hand a
mock-swat. 'You'll give your sons some fancy ideas!'

Alex glanced at Mark who was chewing on a
plastic key and Matthew who was investigating the

ceiling with infantile fervour, his fists waving in the air. He grinned and pulled Carrie tighter in his arms. 'Nothing fancy,' he said. 'Just a plain, ordinary kiss for the woman I love.'

'Alex!' she began warningly, but her face tilted towards his. The babies gurgled and a kettle whistled on the stove, but Carrie was oblivious to anything but Alex's embrace. This was how it always was with them. Passion sprang between them from a secret glance or the mere touch of hands. Their love surpassed any glory she gained from ballet, and Carrie had no regrets. They were partners in a dance of desire: a dance that would last for ever.